"Payback for your past, from my future..."

AF663869

THE ALTERNATE SHADOWS

JITHIN ROY

This is a work of fiction. Names, characters, businesses, places, events and incidents are either products of the author's imagination or used in a fictitious manner. Any resemblance to actual persons, living or dead, or actual events is purely coincidental.

First Edition: March 2025
Printed in India

Printed at Gapmeta Ventures Pvt. Ltd. Navi Mumbai
Typeset in Georgia

ISBN: 978-93-6070-891-7

Cover Design: Rajeev Sakshi

STORYMIRROR
Stories that reflect you

Publisher: StoryMirror Infotech Pvt. Ltd.
Unit No. F/705, 7th Floor Kailas Corporate Lounge,
Veer Savarkar Road, Vikhroli Park Site, Vikhroli West,
Mumbai - 400079, Maharashtra, India.

Web: storymirror.com
Facebook: @storymirror
Instagram: @storymirror
Twitter: @story_mirror
Contact Us: marketing@storymirror.com

Dedication

To the seekers of hidden truths,
who dare to explore the uncharted dimensions of possibility,
where science meets mystery.

To the believers of connections beyond imaginable,
who know the truth is rarely what it seems,
and brave enough to follow the shadows.

To the ones who chase whispers in the dark,
unravel secrets hidden across worlds,
and find truth where none dare to look.

To the ones who navigates through the Shadows of mystery.

This is for you.

ACKNOWLEDGEMENT

At the foremost, Thanks to Almighty.

This book is a testament to the many influences and inspirations that have shaped me, and I am deeply grateful to everyone who has been a part of this journey.

To my parents and sister, who sparked my love for reading and nurtured my curiosity with endless stories—thank you for opening the door to a world of imagination. To my parents especially, for fostering a creative mind unbound by the cages of religion, color, country, or any other limit.

To all my teachers, whose lessons went beyond books and into shaping the storyteller in me.

To my wife, my unwavering pillar of strength, who stood by me with love, belief and patience even when my thoughts wandered far into imaginary realms—your support is my foundation.

And above all, to my kids, who generously shared the time that should have been theirs so that I could bring this tale to life—this book is as much yours as it is mine.

To the thinkers, dreamers, and scientists who explore the boundaries of what we believe to be true—your work has fueled the storyteller inside me.

To my readers, whose curiosity and love for mystery drive me to craft tales worth unraveling—thank you for being in this journey with me.

To **StoryMirror**, my publisher, for believing in this story and helping it find its readers—your faith means the world to me.

To **Chithra Vinayan, Ankita Shibu, Binesh Babu Panicker**, and my son **Evan Roy Varghese**, who gave their time and insight as beta readers—your feedback enriched this work immeasurably.

To **Prashant Reddy Motadoo**, who penned the foreword - your words brought this book to life in ways I could never have imagined.

Finally, to the unsolved mysteries of the universe, for reminding us that the answers often lie just beyond the veil of the known.

With boundless gratitude

Jithin Roy

FOREWORD

I want to begin by saying that this book took me on an unexpected and thought-provoking journey. I had anticipated a gripping crime investigation story, but The Alternate Shadows turned out to be so much more, and what I encountered was something far deeper—something that lingered in my thoughts long after I turned the final page.

It touched on questions I've often asked myself—why do we feel an instant connection with some people we meet for the first time, while with others, there's an unexplained sense of distance? And for the first time, this book offered me an answer—one that satisfies the mind yet simultaneously challenges everything I believed to be real. It forced me to rethink the very nature of reality, blurring the lines between what I know and what I only think I know. This book doesn't just tell a story; it compels you to think, question, and see the world in a new light.

But what makes The Alternate Shadows truly stand out is that it doesn't just explore these questions in an abstract way—it embeds them within a gripping crime thriller that keeps you hooked from the very first chapter. In the vast landscape of crime thrillers, where suspense and intrigue intertwine, 'The Alternate Shadows' emerges as a captivating narrative that challenges perceptions of truth, reality, and the haunting echoes of the past.

Jithin Roy, an engineer-turned-insurance professional with a storyteller's soul, masterfully blends mystery, science, and philosophy into a narrative that is as intellectually stimulating as it is deeply thrilling, pulling the reader into a labyrinth of secrets, hidden rituals, and an investigation that refuses to let go.

Set against the enigmatic backdrop of Kerala, the story follows seasoned police officers Arjun and Manoj, racing against time to decode the chilling trail left by a serial killer wielding an untraceable poison. Their investigation unfolds into a web of interwoven fates, where past and present collide in unexpected ways. With a meticulous blend of crime, corporate intrigue, and deep psychological insight, Jithin constructs a mystery that doesn't just seek resolution—it's about confronting the hidden forces that shape our lives.

Beyond the allure of its mystery, what sets 'The Alternate Shadows' apart is Jithin's fascination with the deeper mysteries of the universe, an element that subtly infuses the narrative with philosophical undertones. His ability to weave the psychological with the procedural, the cosmic with the personal, results in a novel that resonates beyond its final pages.

For readers who revel in the thrill of a well-crafted mystery, who appreciate the delicate dance between fate and justice, and who seek a story that challenges their understanding of truth—this book is a must-read. Jithin's debut into the investigative thriller genre is not just a promising beginning; it is a testament to his storytelling prowess and his unrelenting pursuit of the extraordinary.

As a great writer once said, patience through the first 50 pages of a book is often rewarded—and I assure you, this one is no exception. Give it that much, and you won't just be reading a story; you'll find yourself completely immersed in the world of Arjun, Manoj, Kavitha, Mohit, and Neeta.

Welcome to 'The Alternate Shadows'. Prepare to question everything you think you know.

Prashant Reddy Motadoo
Author of Bestseller book 'Ashwatthama'

PROLOGUE

In the sprawling corridors of the Gupta Regal Group, an air of professionalism pervades every corner, a world filled with sophistication and elegance. This enigmatic environment consumes Neeta's thoughts as she starts her new journey, stepping into the role of secretary for Mohit Gupta—the notorious rebel of the illustrious Gupta lineage. Her eyes wander over the extravagant details of her surroundings, each artifact whispering tales of power and intrigue, just when Shagufta, the receptionist, breaks her chain of thought with her voice.

"Hi Neeta, please follow me to your new desk," Shagufta began, her voice welcoming yet businesslike. "I'll be giving you a general tour of the office. Later, Mr. Mohit's current secretary, whom you'll be replacing, will show you the specifics of your new role."

Neeta managed a smile, her nerves hidden beneath a layer of professionalism. She had worked in similar roles earlier, but this is her first time in such a big firm. "Oh, alright, that sounds great," she replied.

Shagufta continued as they reached the lobby, "You'll need your ID for access around here—I've got it ready for you." She handed Neeta a sleek, metal card. "You'll use lifts A, D, and F to reach Mr. Mohit's floor. This ID will grant you access to those lifts, and the archives, and would also serve as your attendance log."

Stepping into the lift, Neeta found herself jotting down details in her notepad, struggling to keep pace with Shagufta's rapid explanations.

"As for reaching Mr. Mohit's office," Shagufta pointed to a panel in the lift, "the 23rd floor is your stop. Just use your ID here on this scanner."

Neeta, with a trace of reluctance, swipes her ID through the scanner, her movements tentative and unsure. As the card passes through, she catches a glimpse of her own image printed on it, sparking a cascade of what-ifs in her mind. She imagines an alternate self, living out an entirely different story. This kind of daydreaming, a flight from reality, always had a peculiar way of captivating her thoughts especially whenever she was super nervous or super sad.

The soft chime of the elevator abruptly shatters her reverie. They have already reached the 23rd Floor. The doors slide open, and there, in flesh and blood, is Mohit Gupta, the infamous 'Rebel' of the Gupta dynasty. He leans casually against the wall, a toothpick nonchalantly placed between his lips, clad in a suit of the most striking blue color, an embodiment of effortless corporate charisma.

He offers Shagufta a casual smile, igniting an immediate blush on her face. Neeta, witnessing this exchange, finds an unexpected warmth in the atmosphere.

"Hello, Mr. Gupta..." Shagufta manages to stammer out, her voice a mix of respect and fondness.

"Oh, come on Shagufta, you know better— 'Mr. Gupta' is my father. To you, I'm just Mohit," he responds with an easy familiarity.

"Mohit, meet Neeta Joseph, your new secretary. She's taking over Malana's duties," Shagufta introduces, trying to regain her composure.

Mohit's gaze shifts, sweeping over Neeta with an evaluative glance before meeting her eyes with a disarmingly charming smile. It's a smile that seems to convey not just approval but a welcoming into the fold.

"Welcome to the Gupta Regal Group, Neeta." He extends a hand, bridging the gap between employer and employee.

Neeta reaches out, her voice barely above a whisper, "Hello, Mr. Mohit."

His response is immediate, tinged with a friendly admonition, "Do I have to tell you too? Call me Mohit."

The moment is interrupted by Shagufta, who, noting Neeta's bashful grin, suggests, "Mohit, we must proceed. I'll accompany you down and have the driver ready your car if you're leaving?"

"That sounds perfect, Shagufta, thank you," he replies, with a nonchalant grace.

As Mohit steps back into the lift, he throws a final glance, his smile turning devilishly sweet, the kind of smile that could unsettle even the most composed, leaving an indelible mark in the fleeting moment before the doors close.

Neeta and Mohit, nestled together in the cozy confines of Neeta's apartment, found themselves enveloped in laughter and warmth. The memory of their initial encounter seemed both distant and vivid as they sat there, alone, while Neeta's flat-mate was away. Over the past few months, their clandestine meetings had woven a secret relationship of intimacy and understanding, a sanctuary from the world outside. In this hidden haven, Mohit discovered a joy he hadn't known before.

Their story had unfolded from an unlikely beginning—stemming from a bitter altercation within Mohit's family. They had belittled him, declaring he would end up alone, a prophecy that stung with frustration and isolation. Retreating to the solitude of his office, he sought solace in the numbness of alcohol, a desperate attempt to silence the echoes of their words.

It was in this vulnerable state that Neeta found him, her presence like a beacon in his self-imposed darkness. That day marked the first time he truly opened up to someone without fear of judgment or scorn. With Neeta, Mohit found an understanding that transcended the superficial image the world, and he himself had constructed.

He, who had once embraced the role of the indifferent rebellious son, recognized a profound truth—he cared deeply, perhaps more than anyone in his family, but was ensnared by his own inability to express his feelings.

Now, as they sat wrapped in each other's arms, their conversation meandering through memories, Neeta's mind wandered to a familiar contemplation: "What would it be like if I were someone else, in another universe?" This time, however, she voiced the question to Mohit, her curiosity mingling with their shared vulnerability.

"Mohit, do you believe in soulmates?"

Mohit paused, considering her question with a seriousness that matched the depth of their relationship. "I want to believe, and I suppose I do to some extent—but more as a beautiful notion rather than a concrete reality. The concept is entangled in so much religious and scientific debate that it's hard to know what to hold onto. Yet, when it comes to feelings, to the raw essence of human connection... yes, I believe. If soulmates were real, you would undoubtedly be mine, in every life, every universe."

Neeta felt a warmth spread through her as she absorbed his words, then, with a hesitant curiosity, she probed further, "Mohit, what do you think we would be like in another universe?"

Contents

CHAPTER 1

THE PILOT

Kerala Times In-Depth Report: The Enigmatic 'Past & Future' Serial Killer

Date: June 21, 2023

Kochi, Kerala:

In a shocking turn of events, the state is haunted by a mysterious serial killer, leaving residents in a state of fear and confusion. Over the past four months, five seemingly unrelated individuals have fallen victim to this elusive murderer.

What makes these murders even more mysterious is the vigilante-like note left at each crime scene, reading, "Payback for your past from my future." The police department is baffled by the lack of any apparent connections between the victims which adds another layer of complexity to the investigation. This case has not only mystified the Kerala Police but also attracted the nation's attention due to the cryptic and vigilante nature of the crimes.

The list of victims, in the order of the murders, are Subhash Kumar, the owner of a private bank, Alex Mathew, a well-established artist, Dinesh Menon, a famous investigative journalist, Sofiya Ahmed, an IT employee whose body was discovered in Tamil Nadu, indicating that the killer has expanded their hunting grounds beyond Kerala. And now with the addition of Aparna Devi, a politician to the list of victims, this seems to be becoming a high-profile case.

These murders, with their apparent randomness and the lack of clear connections between the victims, are clearly complicating the police's efforts to profile the killer and anticipate future crimes.

For the last 4 months, law enforcement agencies have been scrambling for clues as the state grapples with the terror of an unknown assailant. The Police team, under the guidance of the efficient Crime Branch ACP Manoj Xavier, is in a frantic race against time to decode the killer's messages and stop further bloodshed. Despite the deployment of advanced forensic techniques and extensive manhunts, the police find themselves perennially several steps behind the murderer.

"The complexity of the motives and the meticulous planning of the killer has presented unique challenges," ACP Manoj explained in a recent interview. "Each murder scene is forensically clean with minimal evidence left behind, showcasing a chilling level of premeditation and sophistication."

The serial killings have cast a long shadow over the public's perception of safety. The police force's seeming helplessness in the face of such calculated evil has led to public outcry, with citizens demanding more effective protection and quicker resolution to the crisis.

In response, law enforcement has increased patrols and is closely collaborating with neighboring states to track the killer's movements. Community meetings have been set up to educate the public on safety precautions and the importance of community vigilance.

"Rest assured, we are utilizing every resource at our disposal to apprehend this criminal," ACP Manoj assured the public. "We will not rest until justice is served."

The Kerala Police remain on high alert, and the people of Kerala wait anxiously for a breakthrough in the case that has shaken their community to its core. But the question is -Is it helping? Seems the police force needs to be sharper & more productive.

Deputy Inspector General (DIG) Pankaj Kukreja, sitting in his office in Kochi, was reading the article aloud so that Manoj would also listen. The article's portrayal felt like an outright mockery of the Police Department, and DIG Pankaj, Manoj's direct supervisor, was visibly enraged. Newspapers, TV Channels and social media are filled with news, creative stories and features about the serial killings. Until this moment, DIG Pankaj had maintained a decent opinion of Manoj's capabilities. However, as he glanced over, his eyes were filled with a mix of despair and scorn, clearly not expecting his decision to entrust Manoj with the high-profile case would be wrong.

Manoj had been grappling with the recent murder of Aparna Devi, marking the fifth in a perplexing series of seemingly unrelated killings that had spread a veil of terror across Kerala and Tamil Nadu. Each murder bore the same haunting signature: victims dying due to heart attack, which is assumed to be due to some sort of poisoning with an undetectable toxin, accompanied by a cryptic note chillingly stating, "Payback for your past, from my future."

The killings started in February 2023 and the case was handed over to Manoj in April, after the 3rd murder. Since then, Manoj had dedicated every ounce of his detective prowess to unraveling this intricate case, and now, under the dim June light, he was no closer to identifying the murderer. Manoj has become so obsessive about this case that it has started affecting his personal life also. The leads were scant, the trail cold, and in the oppressive silence of the cabin, only the sound of DIG Pankaj's accusations of investigative inadequacies filled the air, echoing off the walls like a resounding gavel of judgment.

"Manoj, what's happening here? Five murders on your watch, just like that?" DIG Pankaj's voice thundered across the room.

"Sir, I've been working..." Manoj started his voice with a mix of frustration and determination.

"Listen, Manoj!" DIG Pankaj interrupted, but his tone softened. "You're one of our brightest. This case is a beast, but if anyone can crack it, it's you. Solve this before the media turns it into a circus. Remember, your reputation is on the line."

"Yes, sir. I'll handle it," Manoj promised, though doubt lingered in his heart.

Leaving the office, Manoj took a moment to collect himself before retreating to his own space. "A strong filter coffee," he instructed the Peon, needing something to cut through the haze of accusations and pressure.

Sitting alone, the steam from the coffee seemed to carry away his thoughts. DIG Pankaj's words about his team's failure echoed in his head. Shaking off the mental fog, Manoj called upon his team—Inspector Rajiv Das and Inspector Maya Vinod.

"No clear links between the victims," he mused aloud, "but the poison—there's our thread."

"Sir, we need something solid," his second-in-command, Rajiv, reminded him.

"I know, my reputation, our integrity—it's all hanging by a thread," Manoj admitted, feeling the weight of responsibility.

Determined, he decided to revisit the case files with renewed focus, hoping to catch what they had missed. "Let's go over everything again," he declared, not ready to surrender to defeat.

Case Summary File: Past & Future Serial Killings
Updated on 20th June 2023

First Murder

Case Number:	*8134/2023*
Type of Case:	*Homicide*
Date of Registration:	*February 18th, 2023*
Police Station:	*Trivandrum Fort Police Station*
Jurisdiction:	*Trivandrum*

Victim:	*Subhash Kumar*
Age:	*58*
Occupation:	*Private Bank owner*
Reported by:	*Vineeta Subhash, Wife of the deceased*
Accused:	*Yet to be identified*
Date of Incident:	*February 18th, 2023*
Time of Death:	*05:25 PM*
Nature of Offense:	*Homicide, possibly involving poison*

Incident Details:

On the above-mentioned date, the deceased, Subhash Kumar, a private bank owner, was found unresponsive at his residence in Trivandrum. Initially suspected to have suffered a heart attack, the discovery of a note, near the body, with cryptic language indicated foul play. The note, written by a marker on a torn notebook page, read, "Payback for your past, from my future."

Position of the Body:

The body was discovered seated in an armchair in the living room, exhibiting no signs of struggle.

Investigation:

The crime scene was secured and photographed. Witness statements were collected and recorded. Investigative teams from multiple departments were deployed to gather evidence and interview potential witnesses and suspects. Forensic experts analyzed the remains for traces of toxic substances.

Evidence:

Physical Evidence: A note written with marker on a torn notebook page was found near the body.

No signs of physical struggle or tampering at the scene.

Documentary Evidence: Statements from family and neighbors.

Forensic Evidence: Preliminary autopsy indicates a heart attack potentially induced by poison.

Sections Invoked:

Section 302, Indian Penal Code (Murder)

Section 201, Indian Penal Code (Destruction of Evidence, if applicable)

Judicial Orders:

None at this stage.

Final Observations:

The wife of the deceased reported no prior health issues or threats to the deceased.

No evidence of any physical struggle.

Preliminary autopsy suggests a heart attack, potentially induced by some specialized poison. Confirmation of the specifics of the poison used and the method of administration is yet to be determined.

Motive presumed to be revenge.

No significant leads or suspects were identified.

Note: This case is classified as the first murder in the "Past & Future Serial Killings" series.

Second Murder

Case Number: *20131/2023*
Type of Case: *Homicide*
Date of Registration: *March 15, 2023*
Police Station: *Ernakulam South Police Station, Kochi*
Jurisdiction: *Kochi, Kerala*

Name: *Alex Mathew*
Age: *44*
Occupation: *Painting Artist*
Reported By: *Kavitha Pratap, Girlfriend of Alex Mathew*
Accused: *Yet to be identified*

Date of Incident:	*March 15, 2023*
Time of Death:	*01:40 AM*
Nature of Offense:	*Homicide, possibly involving poison*

Incident Details:

On March 15, 2023, Alex Mathew, a painter, was found deceased in his home studio in Kochi. Initially presumed to have succumbed to a heart attack, a freshly opened painter's canvas discovered near the body raised suspicions. The canvas, seemingly received via courier, bore the inscription: "Payback for your past, from my future," indicating a connection to the "Past & Future Serial Killings" case. The victim's girlfriend, Kavitha Pratap, discovered the body and reported the incident to the police control room.

Position of the Body:

The body was found lying on the studio floor, near an easel, with no visible signs of struggle.

Investigation:

The crime scene was secured and photographed. Forensic teams conducted a detailed examination of the crime scene. Potential witnesses and suspects were interrogated and recorded. Forensic experts analyzed the blood samples for traces of toxic substances. Investigators are in the process of gathering additional evidence to uncover the motive and perpetrator.

Evidence:

Physical Evidence: A painter's canvas with the inscription: "Payback for your past, from my future."

Courier packaging was unable to be found. Copy of courier delivery slip collected from the dustbin.

Documentary Evidence: Statements from the victim's girlfriend and acquaintances.

Forensic Evidence: Preliminary autopsy indicates heart attack as the cause of death and the presumed cause to be some sort of poisoning.

Sections Invoked:

Section 302, Indian Penal Code (Murder)
Section 201, Indian Penal Code (Destruction of Evidence, if applicable)

Judicial Orders:

None at this stage.

Final Observations:

Similarities in modus operandi with the earlier case of Subhash Kumar in Trivandrum.

The cryptic note suggests the involvement of the same perpetrator or group.

Investigation continues to trace the courier's origin and uncover the motive, using the copy of the courier delivery slip found.

Motive presumed to be revenge.

No significant leads or suspects were identified.

Third Murder

Case Number:	*16812/2023*
Type of Case:	*Homicide*
Date of Registration:	*April 8, 2023*
Police Station:	*Kottayam East Police Station*
Jurisdiction:	*Kottayam, Kerala*
Name:	*Dinesh Menon*
Age:	*52*
Occupation:	*Reporter*
Reported By:	*Asif Jaffar, Manager and friend*
Accused:	*Yet to be identified*

Date of Incident:	*April 8, 2023*
Time of Death:	*07:35 PM*
Nature of Offense:	*Homicide, possibly involving poison*

Incident Details:

Dinesh Menon, a reporter, was found dead on April 8th, 2023, in Kottayam. A WhatsApp message from an anonymous number, stating "Payback for your past from my future," connected his death to the serial killings. His manager, who discovered the body, notified the police immediately.

Position of the Body:

The body was found slumped over a desk in his office, with no signs of struggle.

Investigation:

A comprehensive forensic examination of the crime scene and victim's body was conducted. The manager, who stays with the deceased, in the same home was subject to deep questioning, but without any results. Potential suspects identified through the victim's professional history were interrogated, but no strong motives were established. The victim's phone and computer were confiscated for further analysis.

Evidence:

Physical Evidence: Victim's phone showing the anonymous message. Office and desk items collected for forensic examination.

Documentary Evidence: Statements from the manager and other close associates.

Forensic Evidence: Preliminary autopsy indicates heart attack as the cause of death

Sections Invoked:

Section 302, Indian Penal Code (Murder)
Section 201, Indian Penal Code (Destruction of Evidence, if applicable)

Judicial Orders:

None at this stage.

Final observations:

The cryptic WhatsApp message connects the case to the ongoing "Past & Future Serial Killings."

Modus operandi consistent with previous murders, indicating a serial killer or organized group.

The anonymous message was traced to a web-based application with some IP-masked system.

Investigation continues to identify the source of the anonymous message and motive.

Cause of death suspected to be poison-induced heart attack.

Toxicology report and forensic analysis didn't provide details of any poison.

Fourth Murder

Case Number: *TN/2023/38137*
Type of Case: *Homicide*
Date of Registration: *May 19, 2023*
Police Station: *T Nagar Police Station*
Jurisdiction: *Chennai, Tamil Nadu*

Name: *Sofiya Ahmed*
Age: *45*
Occupation: *IT Employee*
Reported By: *Ahmed Hussain, Spouse of the deceased*
Accused: *Yet to be identified*

Date of Incident: *May 18, 2023*
Time of Death: *11:18 PM*
Nature of Offense: *Homicide, possibly involving poison*

Incident Details:

On May 19th 2023, law enforcement authorities of Chennai responded to a reported death in Tamil Nadu. Sofiya Ahmed was found deceased in her home in T Nagar, Chennai. Her husband, Ahmed Hussain, discovered the body upon his return from a business trip. Initially, local police deemed the death to be natural; however, the discovery of an email printout near the body bearing the message, "Payback for your past, from my future," linked her death to the ongoing serial killings. The local investigating officer, upon reviewing the evidence, escalated the case to the Kerala Crime Branch, classifying it as the fourth murder in the serial killings.

Position of the Body:

The body was found lying in bed, suggesting Sofiya Ahmed died in her sleep, with no signs of struggle.

Investigation:

The scene was secured and examined by both local police and forensic teams. The Kerala Crime Branch team reached Chennai and did a thorough investigation the next day. Evidence, including the printout of the email, was collected for further analysis. Interviews with the husband, neighbors, colleagues, and friends were conducted. The husband reported no previous threats or unusual behavior.

Evidence:

Physical Evidence: Email printout with the cryptic message found near the body. No signs of physical injury or forced entry into the home.

Documentary Evidence: Statements from the victim's spouse, family members, friends, colleagues, and neighbors.

Forensic Evidence: Autopsy results suggest a heart attack, likely induced by poison. Toxicology tests conducted.

Sections Invoked:

Section 302, Indian Penal Code (Murder)
Section 201, Indian Penal Code (Destruction of Evidence, if applicable)

Judicial Orders:

None at this stage.

Final Observations:

The crime shows similarities with previous serial killings, particularly in the cryptic message and cause of death connecting it to the ongoing "Past & Future Serial Killings."

Cause of death suspected to be poison-induced heart attack.

The email was traced to a web-based application utilizing an IP-masked system, hindering direct identification of the sender.

The Kerala Crime Branch is continuing its investigation, with an emphasis on identifying the perpetrator and uncovering any connections between the victims.

As of date, no specific details regarding the motive or the identity of the perpetrator have been established.

Fifth Murder

Case Number: *23343/2023*
Type of Case: *Suspicious Death (Homicide Investigation)*
Date of Registration: *June 20, 2023*
Police Station: *Calicut Town Police Station*
Jurisdiction: *Calicut, Kerala*

Name: *Aparna Devi*
Age: *43*
Occupation: *Politician*
Reported By: *Vinu Kumar, Driver of Aparna Devi*
Accused: *Yet to be identified*

Date of Incident: *June 20, 2023*
Time of Death: *03:48 PM*
Nature of Offense: *Suspected poisoning leading to cardiac arrest*

Incident Details:

On June 20, 2023, during a journey from Calicut to Kannur for an official meeting, Aparna Devi, a prominent political figure, was discovered deceased in her car. The driver reported the incident after noticing her unresponsive condition in the back seat. This was reported to have occurred while she was traveling for a meeting and just after having lunch at a restaurant. A handwritten note with the ominous message, "Payback for your past, from my future," was found within the vehicle, pointing to its connection with the string of serial killings under investigation.

Position of the Body:

The victim's body was reclined in the rear seat of the vehicle. No signs of physical altercation or disturbance were observed at the scene.

Investigation:

The car was inspected for physical evidence, and the surroundings were secured for forensic analysis. The victim's last meal was traced to a nearby restaurant, which was scrutinized for potential tampering or suspicious activities. The driver was interrogated extensively and has provided a detailed timeline of events. Restaurant staff and patrons present during the victim's meal were also interviewed. Samples from the car, as well as biological specimens from the victim, have been sent for laboratory testing. Surveillance footage from the restaurant and along the route was reviewed for any clues.

Evidence:

Physical Evidence: A handwritten note containing the recurring cryptic message. Receipts and items from the restaurant where the victim had her last meal.

Documentary Evidence: Statements from the driver and restaurant personnel. CCTV recordings from relevant locations.

Forensic Evidence: Preliminary findings suggest a cardiac arrest potentially induced by a toxic substance. Detailed toxicology reports recorded.

Sections Invoked:

Section 302, Indian Penal Code (Murder)
Section 201, Indian Penal Code (Destruction of Evidence, if applicable)
Section 120B, Indian Penal Code (Criminal Conspiracy)

Judicial Orders:

None at this stage.

Final Observations:

The case exhibits similarities with previous incidents in the ongoing serial killings, particularly the method of death and the cryptic message.

Cause of death suspected to be poison-induced heart attack.

No specific details regarding the motive or the identity of the perpetrator have been established.

Efforts are focused on identifying a pattern or connection between the victims to ascertain the perpetrator's motive.

Conclusion Notes:

The pattern of these murders indicates a methodical serial killer with a signature modus operandi involving poison-induced heart attacks and cryptic notes. Despite extensive investigations, the motive and identity of the killer remain elusive. Following the standard interrogation and investigation, individual potential suspects connected to each victim were placed on low priority, with the understanding that serial killings were possibly happening.

The items, assumed to be related to the murders like the vigilante notes, the canvas, laptop, plates, etc., from all the murder locations have been collected and kept in the department evidence room. The poison used leaves no traceable substance but alters blood composition, complicating detection. Efforts are ongoing to decipher the meaning behind the repeated message, "Payback for your past, from my future," and to identify any hidden links between the victims even if in the past. No relationship whatsoever was found yet between the victims. All of different age groups, no common college/schooling, no common workplace, not part of any same clubs, associations, or organizations at any point of time in any of their life, each working in completely different fields. All leading a calm life without any visible harm to others. The case is a top priority one, with investigative teams collaborating with experts to solve these crimes and apprehend the perpetrator.

●●●

Report Prepared by:

Rajiv Das, Inspector & Maya Vinod, Inspector

Signed by:

Manoj Xavier, Assistant Commissioner of Police, Crime Branch, Kochi

Manoj was deeply engrossed in examining the case files, meticulously searching for an elusive clue, when the DIG walked into his cabin with news that would change the trajectory of this case for him.

"Manoj, you've been working hard, but the pressure from above is intense," the DIG explained gravely. "The Chief Minister has intervened, bringing in a specialist from Delhi to lead the case. You're being reassigned."

The news struck Manoj with force, rendering him momentarily speechless. Never before had he been removed from a case. "But Sir, how is this just? I've dedicated every waking hour to solving this, but the leads are like shadows—there but untouchable."

The DIG met his gaze with compassion and a hint of firmness. "I understand your frustration, but orders are orders, coming from the very top. Don't think this reflects poorly on you. You're being prepared for greater responsibilities, Manoj."

With a heavy heart, Manoj acknowledged the directive. "When will this new Officer arrive?"

"In two days. Prepare the necessary files for handover," the DIG instructed, handing Manoj a folder. "By the way, this is his profile. I think you might know him."

Resigned, Manoj took the folder, his feelings a storm of disbelief and resignation.

As he slumped back into his chair, curiosity piqued, he opened the file handed to him by the DIG. His eyes widened in disbelief upon recognizing the name: Arjun Sharma. A surge of nostalgia swept over him as he recalled his old friend from their training days in Delhi, a companion from his own batch.

A smile crept across Manoj's face amidst the turmoil. The prospect of reuniting with Arjun, under such professional circumstances, was unexpectedly comforting. He eagerly anticipated not just a reunion but the opportunity to collaborate on the case that had become his obsession.

Memories of their time together in the academy surfaced, painting a vivid picture of the diligent, earnest Arjun he had known. The thought of working with Arjun brought a rare moment of relief to Manoj's tumultuous day.

In the halls of the police academy, where the scent of discipline and dreams lingered in the air, Arjun and Manoj created a friendship that would stand true to the tests of time. As aspiring officers, their days were filled with tiring training sessions, shared ambitions, and unspoken companionship.

Arjun, with his unwavering determination and charisma, stood out among his peers. His dedication to mastering every aspect of law enforcement was propagative. Despite the rigorous training, Arjun approached each challenge with a smile, turning the most demanding drills into opportunities for companionship.

During those early morning runs and late-night study sessions, Arjun and Manoj became more than just colleagues; they became confidants. His sense of duty was matched only by his sense of humor. Whether navigating the problems of criminal law or cracking a joke to lighten the mood, Arjun was a funny companion.

Manoj and Arjun's bond deepened through shared victories and setbacks. From acing exams to stumbling through their first simulations, Arjun's presence made every experience richer. He wasn't just a friend; he was a pillar of support, pushing Manoj to persevere when the challenges seemed insurmountable.

Arjun's commitment to justice extended beyond the academy walls. His moral compass was resolute, a guiding light for Manoj and himself, as they envisioned futures as defenders of the law. Together, they navigated the intricacies of police work, absorbing the principles that would shape their careers.

In the final days of their graduation, Arjun chose to join the Special Forces while Manoj opted for a career in the Crime Branch. As they graduated as community protectors, the memories of their early years cemented an unbreakable bond between them.

CHAPTER 2

COMPLEX CONNECTIONS

Arjun had recently received directives from his superiors to relocate to Kochi and tackle a highly complex case that had been stirring a significant media frenzy yet remained unresolved for nearly five months. Having received the case files just the previous day, he had dedicated his night to combing through them, all while managing his packing, and preparing to depart immediately. The case was indeed baffling.

The mystery encompassed five murders that had somehow slipped under the radar of the local authorities. He learned that the case was initially handled by the local police and then handed over to the Crime Branch. He was quite surprised to learn that the investigation didn't reach any conclusion even though it was led by ACP Manoj, whom he had great respect for, as he knew from his training period itself. Despite their efforts, there seemed to be crucial elements they had overlooked. Considering this fact, he knew this was going to be a complex and tough case.

Boarding the plane to Kochi, he settled into his seat and began to sift through the documents again, searching for the elusive links, noticing minor yet potentially crucial oversights in each file. He just was eager to catch up with Manoj, discuss about these, and crack this case together.

Upon his arrival in Kochi, a constable was waiting at the airport, ready to escort him to the flat arranged for his stay during the assignment.

Stepping into the enigmatic realm of the "Past & Future Serial Killings Case" was like entering an entirely different universe, one that held Kerala in a tight grip of fear and mystery. Despite his roots in Kerala being his mother's place, this particular town was a bit of an unfamiliar territory for him.

The atmosphere in Kerala, especially post DIG's press conference, was charged with a palpable mix of excitement and curiosity, heightened by the media's relentless coverage. The spotlight on his arrival only intensified the sense of expectation surrounding his involvement in the case.

Having a repertoire of handling cases that strayed far from the ordinary—such as "The Lucid Dream Case", "Subliminal Killings", and "The Sleeper Cell Case"—he was no stranger to complex investigations. Each of these instances had engraved their unique challenges into his career. Now, with the media spotlight turning this investigation into a public spectacle, the stakes were higher than ever.

Upon his arrival at the station, he was greeted by ACP Manoj, a familiar face from his days at the Police Academy. It quickly dawned on him that Manoj had been removed from the very case he was now assigned to lead. The realization brought an uncomfortable sense of guilt over him. Seeking to bridge the awkwardness, he reached out with a gesture of camaraderie.

"Hi, Manoj. It's been ages, what, ten years now since we last crossed paths?" he initiated, trying to lighten the atmosphere.

Manoj responded with a mix of nostalgia and a touch of relief. "Hey Arjun, yeah, it's been a while. I heard that you visited Kerala many times in between for official duties as well as personal purposes, but we were never able to catch up! Anyway, I was actually relieved to hear you were taking over. If anyone can crack this, it's you."

Feeling a pang of sympathy, he said, "I'm truly sorry, Manoj. You know, I was under the impression that we are going to be working together. I didn't know that you are being reassigned. Anyway, you could join my team. I will speak to the DIG"

But Manoj shook his head, a resigned smile on his face. "No, man, I've been sidelined already. Somehow, it's become a personal battle now."

Respecting Manoj's stance, he shifted the conversation towards a lighter note, "How about we catch up over drinks tonight? We could go over old times and maybe you could share some insights on the case."

Arjun's suggestion brought a familiar smile to Manoj's face. "You never change, Arjun! Always mixing work with a bit of fun."

Their laughter echoed a shared history, reminiscent of their academy days when Arjun would sneak in beers during study sessions, much to Manoj's chagrin.

Amid their light-hearted banter, an officer approached Arjun, interrupting their moment. She informed him that the DIG had summoned him for a press conference. With a nod to Manoj, signaling a raincheck on their plans, he followed her, ready to face the media's barrage.

He stepped out of the station into the chaotic glare of camera flashes and the cacophony of reporters bombarding the DIG with questions. In his khaki-colored uniform, he took his place slightly behind the DIG, observing the seasoned officer as he fielded inquiries with poise.

"The investigation has indeed been lengthy," the DIG acknowledged, his voice cutting through the noise. "Despite the accumulation of evidence, we are yet to link it definitively to a suspect, prompting the intervention of Special Investigation Officer Arjun Sharma. We're optimistic about his impact here with his expertise in navigating complex cases." Turning to him, the DIG invited, "Arjun, perhaps you could address some of these questions?"

With a nod, he stepped forward, the incessant shutter clicks marking his transition to the forefront. Amidst the barrage of questions, he requested, “Please, one at a time. It’ll be easier to provide clear answers.” He gestured to a reporter.

“Mr. Arjun, congratulations on your past successes. Can you outline your approach to this perplexing case?” one reporter asked.

Understanding the complexity of the task at hand, he replied, “The intricacy of this case demands innovative thinking, which will be crucial in our approach.”

Another reporter quickly followed up, “Have there been any communications from the perpetrator, anything taunting, perhaps, that could shed light on their identity?”

He shook his head, “We’ve only found notes indicating a motive rooted in vengeance. The messages, cryptic as they are, suggest premeditation and a personal vendetta.”

A concern for public safety was raised next: “With a serial killer still on loose, what measures are being implemented to protect the community?”

He reassured them, “We’re executing all necessary precautions. The nature of these crimes suggests targeted attacks, not random acts, but rest assured, our police force remains on high alert.”

Just then, the DIG leaned in, whispering a strategic retreat, hinting at the risk of the ongoing media engagement compromising their efforts.

Acknowledging his superior’s concern, he addressed the media with finality, “We appreciate your interest, but we must now focus on a new, sensitive lead in the investigation. Details will be shared when appropriate. Thank you.”

With that, they made their exit, shielded by officers from the advancing press, returning to the sanctuary of the station to regroup and advance their inquiry.

That evening, Arjun found himself seated across from Manoj in a quiet bar, a bottle of Tennessee Whiskey between them, his thoughts tunneling solely into the unresolved queries of the day.

Manoj broke the silence," How's Divya doing? Heard you are quite often travelling to Dubai to visit her! Why don't you two get married? It's almost 15 years now, right?

Arjun replied with his naughty smile," We both love and are committed to each other, but we are not marriage materials, you know? We both are so much into our jobs and don't want to be a burden to each other. So, this long-distance live-in relationship is the best. And you can see that it's working for us. See, now I am full on my investigative work and she's the director of a prominent firm in Dubai. It's a win-win for us". He continued, " Unfortunately, you can't experiment with this now as you already missed that chance". Both laughed on this for a bit.

"What stopped you from joining the Special Investigation Team, Manoj?" Arjun probed, after a bit of silence, unable to mask his curiosity.

Manoj took a moment, then revealed, "It's nothing against you. Truth is, I'm still on this case, just unofficially now. Officially off the roster or not, I need to see this through."

Arjun nodded, understandingly, "Then, let's do this together. You and me. Off the books. This case seems to be a labyrinth; mutual updates might just be what we need."

Manoj agreed, "That could work. If I need anything—lab results or such—I'll pass them through you. Also, I suggest putting Inspectors Rajiv and Maya in your team. Both are very good and will gel with your style. Further, they had been with me from the start of this case."

With a mutual understanding, they dived into the case details, Manoj sharing his insights and hypotheses. As the night wore on and their conversation began to wind down, Manoj glanced at his watch.

"Looks like it's late, I should head out."

Arjun teased, "What? It's barely past eleven. The night's just getting started."

But Manoj was firm, “Yeah, but it’s dark out, time for me to go.”

Arjun let out a laugh as Manoj departed, “Alright, take care. See you tomorrow.”

With a light-hearted jibe, Manoj retorted, “Just don’t go overboard here, alright?”

As Manoj left, Arjun migrated to the bar, his gaze inadvertently catching a woman in a green dress, maybe around 27-28 years old, moving rhythmically on the dance floor, her aura mesmerizing. Her gaze met his, filled with an intriguing blend of confidence and allure, tempting yet foreign to his disciplined life. She seemed quite familiar to him, like someone he had known for a long time.

Being a handsome and attractive guy, he is no new to getting such glances from girls. But Arjun always maintains a committed relationship with Divya, his girlfriend. Despite the distance and challenges, he remains loyal to her, resisting temptations that could jeopardize their bond. This steadfastness highlights his dedication not just in his professional life, but in his personal affairs as well.

Lost in contemplation, he was startled when the bartender slid a glass of Tennessee Tea towards him, “I didn’t order this.”

“It’s from her,” the bartender indicated, nodding towards the woman nearby—the very one from the dance floor.

Acknowledging the gesture, Arjun raised his glass to her, maintaining his reserve. She approached, the same compelling gaze locking with his.

“Is this seat taken?” she asked, a hint of intrigue in her voice.

“No, but this might not be the best idea,” Arjun cautiously responded.

Her reply, laced with a playful curiosity, broke through his defenses, “Not even for a fan? I’m Kavitha.”

CHAPTER 3

VEILED ENCOUNTERS

Kavitha was heading to Alex's apartment to spend the holiday with him. As she had been too busy with her research and due to which she hadn't been able to see him during the entire week. On her day off they would generally do some lazy lunches, movie nights, and lay in bed either cuddling or talking all day.

Alex had been having a hard week. He was sick a lot due to the fever that just won't heal even though it had been eight days and now that he was feeling better Kavitha decided to make this day his. Even though there was a big age difference it never affected their relationship, as they were connected through their intense passion for painting and music.

She went by the flower store to get some flowers and then went to get some appam and egg roast from 'Kochi Kitchen Restaurant', which was Alex's favorite. As she walked up the stairs, she was filled with anticipation of spending this day with him. She reached his door, rang the bell, and waited for him to open. She started scrolling on her phone, and after a few minutes, she called him which he did not receive. She felt something bad was about to happen so she checked her purse & tried to find the keys to his apartment and open the door.

She hadn't spoken to him all morning and thought she would give him a surprise- but as she entered the apartment, she was shocked.

In her own statement given to the police: "I saw Alex's phone ringing next to him where he had fallen and was foaming at his mouth lying awfully still. I checked his breath and then his pulse and both had ceased! My life stopped and all I could do was scream, as all my dreams were shattered at that moment."

On March 15th, her world was irrevocably altered. Three months had passed, yet she scarcely spent time on anything else, her life consumed by the pursuit of justice for her boyfriend's unsolved murder. Her days oscillated between laborious research in her lab and some brief trips outside the villa – her home cum lab, to the nearby supermarket for essentials and her chemicals supplier for lab supplies. But, the most significant journeys she embarked on was the mental traversal, seeking answers hidden in the fabric of the universe.

She would often pause in her once-shared apartment, surrounded by remnants of a life with Alex. She had kept the apartment intact as per the police instruction or maybe because she wanted to see it the way Alex lived in. And today, during one of such visits, she was sitting on the sofa, lost in her daydreams with the background noise of the television barely registering until a significant announcement captured her attention. The police department has assigned a new officer, Arjun Sharma, to lead the investigation into the series of mysterious murders, one of which had claimed Alex.

Snapped back to reality by the news, and spotting Arjun in the press conference video on TV, she gave a devilish smile, as if expecting this moment or more like she was waiting to find him. She quickly sought more information about Arjun Sharma. His profile revealed an experienced and expert special operations officer well known for his out-of-the-box methods, an alumnus of the police academy alongside the previous investigator. Knowledge gleaned from her research hinted at his regular haunts, including a local bar known as "The Black Rock" where he often unwound on weekends, whenever he is visiting Kochi.

Resolved to meet Arjun and perhaps influence the direction of the inquiry, she opted for a subtle approach rather than a direct confrontation. Slipping into her favored green sequin dress, she set out to "The Black Rock", fortifying herself with a drink upon arrival for courage. Somehow, she felt certain he would be there tonight.

At the bar, she spotted Arjun in conversation with the previous case officer, Manoj, which she was least expecting. After downing her drink, she took to the dance floor to steady her nerves, momentarily losing herself in the music and momentarily forgetting the grave reason behind her visit.

Eventually, she regained her composure and turned to find Arjun alone, his gaze locked onto hers. Even though she was sure that he would be feeling connected to her, it seemed fortune was also on her side that evening.

Gathering every ounce of poise within her, Kavitha let the rhythm guide her movements, aware of Arjun's gaze locked onto her. She sensed his scrutiny, yet also noted a distant glaze in his eyes, hinting at a mind burdened with thoughts far from the dance floor. Seizing the opportunity, she approached the bar's end and requested the bartender to send Arjun some special cocktail with what he was having, her treat.

"Could you send him a Tennessee Tea please? And add it to my tab, please."

With a nod, the bartender prepared and slid the drink towards Arjun, jolting him back to the present.

"I didn't order this," Arjun remarked, a touch of surprise in his tone.

The bartender gestured towards Kavitha, "It's from her."

Catching her gaze, a spark of recognition flickered in Arjun's eyes as he acknowledged her gesture with a nod and tasted the drink.

Closing the distance, Kavitha approached with a cautious, hopeful smile. "Is this seat taken?"

Arjun met her with a wary look, "No, but this might not be the best idea."

She lightly countered, "Not even for a Fan? You just seem caught up in your thoughts. Care to share with a semi-stranger?"

He sighed, the professional facade slightly cracking, "It's complex. And while you seem familiar..."

Cutting him off, Kavitha introduced herself, "I'm Kavitha. And you're working on something painfully personal to me."

Recognition dawned on him, "Kavitha... Kavitha Pratap, connected to Alex?"

She confirmed with a nod, her eyes betraying her grief and resolve. "Yes, Alex was my world. I'm seeking the truth behind his demise. I heard you're leading the investigation now."

Arjun's expression softened into one of professional empathy, "I'm truly sorry. It's a tough case, scant on leads."

"That's just it," she pressed on, "I've been gathering some information myself. Perhaps we could pool our resources. I need to know who took Alex from me."

Arjun regarded her, a blend of caution and compassion evident. "I sympathize with your quest for answers. I must tread carefully, but I'm open to hearing what you've uncovered."

Relieved, Kavitha offered her contact details, "I understand. Let's discuss this away from prying eyes. Here's my number; call me tomorrow, and we can meet over breakfast?"

Arjun accepted the card, his demeanor reflecting a newfound determination mingled with understanding.

After Kavitha left, he called Inspector Rajiv and instructed him to collect all the details about Kavitha and send it to him immediately. He was no different from the sharpest police officers who wouldn't trust people that easily.

CHAPTER 4

THE UNFAMILIAR PATH

Arjun left the bar that night with a whirlwind of thoughts. By the time he reached home, he got the mail from Rajiv with the details on Kavitha.

Kavitha Pratap, in her 30s, is an accomplished engineer with degrees in electronics and mechatronics along with a postgraduation in chemical engineering. Arjun just glanced through a big lot of certifications and courses in a wide range of subjects including psychology, Pharmacokinetics, Physics, Neurobiology, and so on, which she did within this young age. She blends her technical expertise with a passion for the arts, excelling as a writer, caricaturist, and cartoonist. Her affluent background allows her the freedom to pursue her diverse interests without financial worry, filling her home with beautiful pencil drawings and caricatures. Her creative and intellectual pursuits showcase her dynamic personality and genius. Currently, she is working towards her PhD at a well- known university based in Australia. Arjun went through all the details, but found nothing suspicious.

What could Kavitha have discovered that had eluded the entire police department? The notion nagged at him, suggesting that perhaps she was withholding critical information, possibly readying for a private confession.

Come morning, still wrestling with these thoughts, Arjun texted Kavitha, inquiring about a possible meeting before his workday began. Her affirmative response, coupled with an invitation to her house, implied significant revelations awaited him.

Arjun reflected on Kavitha's plight as he prepared to leave – the pain of finding love only for it to be snatched away by a merciless killer. He pondered the emotional toll it must have taken on her, now propelled by a drive to unravel the truth behind her boyfriend's murder.

Driving towards Kavitha's residence, Arjun noticed the upscale neighborhood, a stark contrast to the usual environs he patrolled. He arrived at a striking villa, stepping into an ambiance filled with the comforting scent of filter coffee and a semblance of normalcy despite the circumstances.

The guest room was kept very clean and organized. The maid received him and guided him to the living room, which was a complete contrast to the first one. It was like a place where a mutiny had taken place with every bit unorganized in an organized way. It was strewn with papers, a lot of papers - handwritten as well as printouts of digital data. On one side, there was a collection of electronic equipment including a super computer-like thing connected to 2 big screen monitors, an ECG machine-type equipment, and a small desk with tools and materials that looked like an old model watch repair shop. And on another side, there was a small chemistry lab set up with lots of pieces of equipment and a couple of glass jars with chemicals labeled and named neatly. Surprisingly, on the walls as well as among the papers on the floor and table, there were many caricatures-like pencil drawings. Surprisingly, Arjun saw a drawing of a face that was very similar to himself but he decided to ask about that later.

Inside, Kavitha was so engrossed in her research that she didn't even notice Arjun enter, signaling her deep dive into realms beyond conventional policing. Her demeanor was a mix of intense focus and underlying sorrow, a testament to the dual life she now led – one in reality and the other in her investigative world.

"Hey, Kavita! Sorry for the delay; traffic was a nightmare," Arjun began, attempting to break the ice amidst the tense atmosphere.

Kavitha acknowledged him with a nod, her warmth shadowed by the gravity of their meeting. "It's fine, Arjun. I'm just glad you're here. Take a seat," she invited, indicating a space cleared amidst her makeshift workstation. So calm and collected, Arjun thought, her behavior today is like it's 360 degrees different from yesterday's.

Arjun asked, "What's with the drawings? Don't tell me that you are an artist too!"

Kavitha, continuing in a serious tone, answered," Yes, you are right, I am an artist too, a good one, I think. And this is how I got connected to my Alex".

Arjun observed the chaos of her research, evidence of her relentless pursuit. "This all looks pretty intense. A new project?" he ventured, hoping to navigate gently into their discussion.

She exhaled; the weight of her findings evident. "This is far from just a project, Arjun. I've stumbled upon something... unconventional."

The term piqued Arjun's interest, urging him closer. "Unconventional how?" he asked, his skepticism tempered by genuine intrigue.

Kavitha locked eyes with him, the storm within her visible. "I've been working on something significant, Arjun. And it requires an open mind," she implored.

Arjun was taken aback by the gravity in her tone. "Always. What's going on?"

She paused, collecting her thoughts. "I've made a breakthrough in my research, something that could change everything we understand about our reality. And it could help your case to find the killer."

The mention of the case sent a jolt through him. Arjun leaned in further, his attention now fully captivated. "I'm listening."

She didn't want to beat around the bush and wanted to jump straight into the subject in her usual way. But knowing that she is going to disclose something unusual and difficult to comprehend for even a person like Arjun, made her take a step back and do it gradually.

She started with a question, "I am sure of your knowledge about our universe, milky-way and all, from your school books and that this is just one of the universes that exist. Have you ever thought deep into that?" Without waiting for an answer from Arjun, she continued, "What's is your view about alternate universes or universes that exist parallelly with the one we are living in?"

Arjun sat and kept staring at her like she was talking in some anonymous language. And after a break, he spoke, "I'm... I don't know. I remember reading somewhere about the hypothesis on the co-existence of alternate universes, but nothing more. And, there were some case studies I have done where the 'involuntarily slipping into a parallel universe' was given as the reason for some mysterious disappearances, and that reason, I was quite skeptical about."

Kavitha interrupted, "Good that you have read about that. I am also not sure about a person physically slipping into a parallel world or that's out of the scope of my studies. Rephrasing my question, What's your take on any connection with our soul or scientifically the consciousness, in parallel universes?"

"About the soul or consciousness part you mentioned, I don't have a clue about! Do those actually even exist?"

Kavita nodded confirming, "See Arjun, this is my research subject or rather my life's work, and I can vouch for that." She added.

Arjun couldn't stop himself from showing the surprise on his face," Frankly, this is something new to me. And of course, I am not able to comprehend it completely. Can you explain it in layman's terms please"?

Kavitha closed her eyes briefly, focusing on simplifying such a complex concept into terms the average person could understand.

Arjun wanted to break the silence as he was getting a bit impatient because of this, but he chose to give it a shot noting that she is trying to work out something in her mind for the explanation.

After a couple of minutes, she broke the silence in the room with a deep breath and started talking, "See Arjun, Consciousness is the state of being aware of and able to think about one's own existence, sensations, thoughts, and surroundings, or in simple words consciousness is basically being aware of yourself and the world around you. It's what makes you feel like you."

"That part at least I think I know," Arjun said.

She continued, after taking a 2 second break for Arjun to follow, "Now to understand the brain-consciousness connection, we can consider the brain as the biological organ that supports consciousness. From a scientific standpoint, consciousness is often considered an emergent property of the brain's complex neural networks. This means that while consciousness arises from neural activity, it is not reducible to it. Hope you got it."

Arjun just nodded his head mechanically in agreement, even though his mind was still lagging behind in processing what she mentioned.

Seeing the nod, Kavitha smiled and continued, "Good. Now, coming to the concept of multiple universes, or the multiverse, it suggests the existence of parallel universes alongside our own. Each universe could have different physical laws, constants, timelines, and alternate versions of ourselves. Imagine there are many versions of you in different universes, each living a completely different life."

Arjun somehow collected himself together and spoke, "Ok. So, I agree that this is a big piece of knowledge. But how is it going to help the investigation? Can you come to that point, please?"

"You have to wait a bit more to come to that point. But now, just listen to me carefully. I'm going to tell you something which I have never disclosed to anyone, till date. After doing a bit of research about you, I think I can trust you with this. Or rather, I need to tell you this to find who took my Alex away from me," Kavita took a deep, steadying breath. "I've developed a way to travel to alternate universes, Arjun. Parallel dimensions that exist alongside ours."

Arjun's eyebrows shot up in disbelief. Despite his best efforts to maintain an open demeanor, skepticism seeped into his thoughts. "So, you're telling me you've actually built something... to travel to alternate universes?"

"Yes. I know how it sounds, but I've dedicated my research to this. It's not fiction; it's based on solid scientific principles."

But he was already shaking as disbelief clouded his judgment. "Kavitha, come on! This sounds like a plot straight out of a science fiction novel."

Her face fell, and she looked away, hurt evident in her posture. "I expected better from you, Arjun. It's disappointing to see that you're also among those who dismiss things just because they don't understand them. This is like people dismissing and laughing at the idea of Television before 1920 or the telephone before 1876!"

"Look, I'm sorry, Kavitha. I didn't mean to belittle your work. It's just a lot to take in all at once," he said, realizing his mistake and trying to mend the fracture he'd caused.

"To understand this, you need to grasp the concept of multiverses. As I mentioned earlier, they aren't just fictional; they're a part of our reality, beyond our usual perception."

"Okay, I'm listening. But this is... a lot."

"In the simplest terms, when we sleep here, in this universe, our consciousness could wake up in multiple alternate universes and vice versa."

"Wait. How can that happen as sleep time varies in each universe? Are you telling me that the daytime of the alternate version of a person in an alternate universe will be equivalent to the sleep time in this universe? How is that practical?"

"See Arjun, like the time gap between certain countries, there is a time gap between different universes. I have experienced this through my various journeys. So, I would say that the day and night correlation in multiple universes is not exactly proportional. The main point is that it's like living parallel lives, unaware of each other."

"Ok, and you believe this connection exists between all versions of ourselves across universes?"

"Exactly. And not just us, but everyone. Your friends and family all have their counterparts, but the relationships will differ from universe to universe. It's just that any two persons who are connected to each other in any of the universe in whatever way will be connected in all the alternate universes also in the same depth, but through similar or different relationships. For example, you and your father in this universe are closely connected. So, in the alternate universes also, he will be so close to you may be as your close friend, brother, colleague, etc. And sometimes, under certain conditions, we can feel the connections, the echoes from our other lives. Like, you feel so much familiarity – may be a positive feeling or a negative feeling towards someone when you meet them for the first time."

Arjun nodded in agreement with a tint of surprise on his face.

She continued," It's because that person is already connected to you in one of the alternate universes. In short, all our connections have reflections in all the parallel universes."

"Soul connections, across dimensions? This is... beyond anything I've dealt with."

"I know it's hard to digest. However, I can provide you with the scientific explanations and maybe the evidence also." She continued to explain, "As per my theory, quantum processes within the brain play a role in consciousness and that consciousness might involve quantum coherence and entanglement at the microtubular level within neurons. As consciousness has a quantum component, it explains how it can transfer between universes, as quantum states can exhibit non-local behavior. And this process involves aligning the quantum state of the brain's neural network in our universe with a counterpart in the alternate universe. Such alignment would allow the transfer of the conscious state without physical displacement."

"Here, look at this," She took out a box. "These are the devices and injections I've created for the travel. They're designed to allow you to maintain your consciousness as you transition between universes. In simple terms, your brain creates your awareness, and I have found a way to move that awareness to another version of you in a different universe. This lets you wake up there, feeling like the same person, but living a different version of your life. Meanwhile, your brain in this universe enters a semi-restful state, ensuring a smooth and safe transition."

"This explanation helps! Now, you've tried this?" Arjun asked.

"Yes, many times. To different alternate universes. It was... disorienting initially. The Kavitha in that universe had a very different life. It caused suspicion among those around her... me... us. After a couple of visits, I was able to at least gel into my alternate personality to some extent so that I don't create suspicion among others." Kavitha replied.

"I can't even begin to imagine. But, again the same question I have, how does this relate to the case? How will this help in finding the killer of your boyfriend?"

"In alternate universes, people's lives take different paths based on different choices and events. But there's a pattern, a correlation. If we can understand the relationship between the victims and the murderer there, we might find clues in the alternate universe that are non-existent in ours."

"You're saying the killer's alternate self might expose motives or behaviors we can't see in our world?" Arjun asked with eagerness.

"Precisely. Not only the killer's, but the victim's alternate self also starts showing behavioral changes in alternate universes like one of them feeling scared, hatred or submissive towards the other, once a murder takes place in one universe. And it's not just about finding the murderer. It's about understanding the ripple effects of actions across universes. How the act of murder alters the killer's or victim's life path, and how the absence of the victim affects the cosmic balance."

"This... This is a lot, Kavitha. I need some time to process this."

"I understand. It's not something you can accept without evidence. Here, take these printouts. These contain my research thesis, hypothesis, scientific explanations, experiments, and results analysis. Go through them at your own pace. When you're ready, if you believe me, call me. We can discuss how to proceed. It's okay, Arjun. I know how outlandish it sounds. Just read through the detailed studies and explanations, and then we can talk."

"Yes, I'll see you again after I'm done processing. But for now, in this universe, I am getting late for work so I'll see you later!"

After leaving her villa and settling into his car, Arjun replayed their conversation in his mind. He recalled the look in her eyes—she truly believed every word she said; none of it felt fabricated. Taking the papers, he gave them a quick scan and even that brief glance was enough to leave his mind reeling.

It used words like Quantum Entanglement and Temporal Resonance Field which were completely out of his vocabulary. For the time being, he got himself out of the 'alternate universe' mindset and got ready to go to the station so he can dive in and get to work on the case.

As he reached the station the DIG found him coming out of the break room.

"Arjun!"

"DIG Sir, tell me what can I do for you?"

"How far along have you come in your research about the case? What do you think about it?"

"I had a read of everything. I'll be visiting the locations and checking them out this week."

"Okay great! But you need to act a bit fast. The recent murder being that of a politician, the situation is getting bad. Need to close this as soon as possible."

"Sure Sir!"

Arjun left to sit in his cabin and shut the door for some silence to zone into work.

CHAPTER 5

PUZZLE OF THE POISONED BLOOD

Manoj stood in the cold, echoing room, the forensic reports splayed before him like a cryptic map to an unsolved mystery. The atmosphere was laden with the heavy silence that accompanies unresolved tragedies.

The poison, a phantom in their midst, had stealthily claimed five lives, leaving a bewildering trail of questions in its wake. The forensic expert, a seasoned professional worn by the day's challenges, faced Manoj with a look that mingled knowledge with defeat.

"Doctor, what's the latest on the poison analysis?" Manoj inquired, his voice tinged with a mix of hope and desperation.

Dr. Varma, the forensic expert, exhaled deeply. "Manoj, we're hitting walls here. The compound's integration into the victims' systems is unprecedented. It's as if it was designed to be undetectable post-assimilation."

Manoj's mind raced. "Is there no way to isolate this compound? There has to be an angle we haven't explored yet."

A fleeting spark of possibility flickered in Manoj's eyes. "We have tried all the options available to isolate the chemical, but with no success. Now, the only way left to find the chemical composition is, if we had access to the substance before it merged with the bloodstream. But Manoj, finding such a sample now would be nearly impossible without more to go on."

Manoj's brief surge of anger at the lack of progress dissolved as quickly as it had appeared, replaced by a sobering realization of their daunting task.

"There must be something we're missing," Manoj persisted, clinging to the hope of uncovering a new lead. "Have we examined other bodily tissues for residual traces?"

Dr. Varma shook his head. "We've been thorough. The poison's rapid action was indiscriminate, marking its presence throughout the body without a discernible point of entry. What we need is the original delivery method—a syringe, a vial—something that directly administered the toxin."

Manoj considered another angle. "And if the administration was external, perhaps through ingestion?"

"We don't know yet, Manoj. In fact, in none of the victims, we were able to find any concessions in their bodies whatsoever. So, to be open with you, we are yet to find how the poison was administered."

"The conundrum there," Manoj replied, "as I understood, is the absence of the poison in the digestive tract of Dinesh. It's in the bloodstream but bypasses the natural ingestion paths. It defies typical forensic patterns, suggesting a sophisticated, direct-to-bloodstream method. That's why I requested further analysis of the samples collected from the body of Dinesh. Anything on that?"

The conversation took an unexpected turn when Dr. Varma mentioned the secondary finding in the autopsy report. "I totally forgot to update you about that. Not sure if this is of any use. But interestingly, there was a trace of marijuana in the victim's system. It seems unrelated to the cause of death, but it's a peculiar detail."

Manoj raised an eyebrow, processing the new information. "Marijuana? That's odd. It doesn't fit the narrative we've built around Dinesh's lifestyle. Are we missing a piece of the puzzle?"

Doctor Varma nodded, tapping his pen thoughtfully on the table. "It's a curious finding indeed. The drug itself isn't linked to the toxin that killed him. But it raises questions about his activities and associations we might not have considered."

"The meticulous nature of this act... it's chilling," Manoj mused aloud, more to himself than to Dr. Varma. "It's as if the perpetrator was taunting us, deliberately leaving a trail that's cold by design."

Dr. Varma agreed, his voice laced with a mix of excitement and intrigue. "Exactly Manoj. The level of knowledge and precision in this... It's far from the work of an amateur. We're clearly missing something."

Feeling a renewed sense of purpose, Manoj stood up decisively. "I'm going back to Dinesh's place. There has to be something we overlooked. This new detail about the marijuana... it might just change the context of everything."

Doctor Varma gave a supportive nod. "Every detail counts, Manoj. We've hit a wall here, and any piece of new evidence could be the breakthrough we need. Re-examining the crime scene might just shed light on this enigma."

With a mutual understanding of the stakes at hand, Manoj left the sterile confines of the forensic lab, the weight of their conversation fueling a renewed determination to pierce the veil of secrecy surrounding the elusive poison and its mastermind.

The critical piece of evidence in this perplexing case was the sinister reality that the poison had infiltrated every part of the victim's bloodstream, heralding a prolonged and torturous demise. Dinesh, the victim, wasn't just any individual; he was a reporter famed for delving into the murky depths of society, bringing to light stories shrouded in secrecy. Despite the traces of marijuana found in his system, none were discovered in his home, a fact that clashed with the evidence and fueled Manoj's suspicion.

Compelled by a nagging instinct sharpened by years of police work, Manoj, wrestling with his thoughts and theories, decided to revisit the somber confines of Dinesh's apartment. He reached his office, made some calls, and left immediately for Kottayam. His visit wasn't solitary this time; he was accompanied by a police dog, specially trained to detect drugs, hoping to uncover what human eyes might miss.

As they entered, the ambiance of the apartment shifted palpably. A profound silence enveloped them, heavy with the echoes of untold stories and unexposed secrets. The police dog's behavior changed markedly, instantly tense and vigilant, a change Manoj noted as they stepped deeper into the living space.

Ignoring the instinct to survey the entire apartment, Manoj focused on the living room, driven by the dog's unyielding attention towards a large mirror. The animal's growing restlessness and sharp barks offered a stark contrast to the pervading silence, drawing his attention to the seemingly mundane object.

Approaching the mirror, Manoj examined it meticulously, expecting to unveil some hidden aspect that had previously eluded detection. However, the mirror initially offered no clues, standing innocently in the room.

Yet, spurred by rising frustration and the oppressive ambiance, Manoj's restraint shattered along with the mirror as he struck it in a fleeting surge of anger. The broken mirror revealed a clandestine reality – a concealed locker ingeniously crafted into the wall; its contents now laid bare due to Manoj's impulsive act.

Inside the locker lay the disparate elements of Dinesh's hidden life: packets of marijuana, a collection of smoking tools, aged documents neatly stapled into bunches, and some photographs. One of the bunches with 2-3 photographs seemed like an unpublished news feature, whereas others were just some paper cuttings and old college photos and certificates. The printed article along with photos captured Manoj's attention – "The Dark Side of Our Advanced

World." His pulse quickened as he unfolded the papers, uncovering an account of Dinesh's risky investigation into a clandestine black magic gathering in a secluded village. This exploration, fraught with danger, illuminated grim practices that are being carried out even with all the technological advancements happening around. He started reading the report.

The Dark Side of Our Advanced World
Allookkara, Ernakulam District, Kerala
10th July 2003

In the shadows of our seemingly advanced world lies a realm shrouded in darkness, where superstition reigns and black magic thrives. In a remote part of the Allookkara village near Udayamperoor nestled deep within the heart of Kerala and tucked away from the prying eyes of modernity, I ventured into a world that sent shivers down my spine, a world where desires are whispered to the gods in exchange for blood and sacrifice.

As a seasoned investigative journalist, I ventured into this uncharted territory, driven by an insatiable thirst for truth. The agents scattered across the globe, accessible only through trusted references, held the key to unlocking the iron door to this realm. What I encountered surpassed even my darkest imaginings, plunging me into a world where the boundaries between reality and the occult blur with chilling clarity.

My journey into this foreboding realm began with a chill that crept up my spine as I crossed the threshold into a world where black magic reigned supreme. Upon my arrival, I was greeted by a landscape steeped in fear and apprehension. Allookkara was no ordinary village; it was a veritable emporium of forbidden desires, where the desperate sought solace in rituals that promised the fulfillment of their deepest wishes. From love to wealth, health to vengeance, the offerings of black magic knew no bounds.

Guided by an unyielding determination to unearth the truth, I immersed myself in the heart of this clandestine world, posing as a believer in search of fulfillment. Yet, as I delved deeper, I found myself ensnared in a web of deceit and manipulation, where the innocents were exploited and lives hung in the balance.

Participating in a ritual meant to realize the deepest desires of its participants, I stood, cloaked in the guise of faith, as the air crackled with anticipation. Alongside six other participants, I stood in a circle of white-clad figures, our palms marked with symbols of arcane power. Before us lay an altar adorned with swords, suspended precariously above a small bed where a young girl lay, her innocence a stark contrast to the grim tableau unfolding around her.

As the chants of mantras filled the air, a sense of unease settled upon me—a gnawing fear that grew with each passing moment. And then, in a flash of heat and fury, tragedy struck—a thread snapped, and a sword fell, claiming the life of the innocent girl before our horrified eyes.

In the aftermath of this chilling event, the priests' voices rang out with chilling authority, commanding us to remain silent, lest we incur the wrath of ancient curses. The priests, unaffected by the tragedy they had wrought, continued their rites with a cold detachment that sent shivers down my spine. Their assurances rang hollow in the face of such senseless loss, as they dismissed the girl's death as a mere inconvenience, a blip on the radar of their arcane pursuits. Yet, amidst the fear and confusion, a single question burned within me—how could such unspeakable horrors be allowed to persist unchecked?

Returning to the nearby villages in the coming days, I uncovered a web of deception and exploitation that stretched far beyond the confines of Allookkara. Small girls, plucked from the arms of poverty and orphanhood, became pawns in a deadly game of ritual sacrifice, their lives extinguished in service to the insatiable appetites of those who sought power at any cost.

As I reflect on my journey into the heart of darkness, I am haunted by the memory of the girl whose life was snuffed out in the name of superstition and greed. May her story serve as a beacon of light in our collective quest for truth and justice, and may we never forget the cost of silence in the face of evil.

In the end, it is not just the darkness we must confront, but the light within ourselves that guides us towards a better tomorrow. This narrative, emerging like a whisper from the darkness, stands as a solemn reminder, prompting us to contemplate the path we choose in our relentless pursuit of advancement and success."

The narrative struck a chord of chilling familiarity for Manoj.

It brought to mind a suicide note discovered during their early training – a haunting confession from a tormented individual who, after taking part and witnessing a similar horror, could no longer bear the weight of the grief and chose to end his life.

Manoj strained to recall the dates mentioned in the report and the suicide note, realizing they might be pieces of a larger, more sinister puzzle. He called one of his batchmates, who is still in Mumbai, and requested him to take out and send the details of that case. The growing sense of urgency shifted their focus to the photographs found within the locker, which depicted a disturbing scene: a girl at the center of a ritualistic altar, encircled by shadowy figures and ominous symbols. Likely taken through a concealed lens, the images held potential leads on the identities of those involved, yet were frustratingly unclear.

Determined to uncover the truth, Manoj sent the photographs to the technical team, instructing them to use all available means to clarify the images. Concurrently, they forwarded the marijuana samples to the laboratory, suspecting they might contain more than typical contaminants, perhaps even the undetectable poison responsible for Dinesh's demise.

The search for solid evidence and eyewitness testimony proved fruitless. The case was shrouded by a wall of silence, reinforced by time and a shared fear of retaliation. Manoj departed the scene with more questions than answers, the echoes of the past lingering long after they left.

Back at home, the unsolved case weighed heavily upon Manoj. He wanted to just unwind for today. He took a bottle of beer and sat on his sofa trying not to think about this case for a moment. Ironically, a WhatsApp message came from his batchmate informing him that a copy of the Final Report, of the requested case had been mailed.

He took out the laptop and opened the mail. He started reading the details of the case of the suicide of Prof. Amit Mathur.

Case Final Report

Case Number: *MPD1500/0234/2013*
Date: *05 July 2013*
Subject: *Suicide of Professor Amit Mathur*

Incident Details: On 18 June 2013 the Borivali Police Station responded to a call reporting the discovery of a deceased individual at No. 1103, Espree Tower, Borivali West, Mumbai. Upon arrival at the scene, officers identified the deceased as Professor Amit Mathur, aged 44. The time of death was determined to be 09:19 AM.

Investigation: A comprehensive search of the apartment was conducted, revealing a poison bottle. The bottle was promptly collected and submitted for forensic analysis. Additionally, a forensic team thoroughly examined the premises for any further evidence related to the incident.

Forensic Analysis: Results from the forensic analysis confirmed the presence of the same poison found in the bottle within Professor Mathur's system, indicating ingestion. No signs of forced entry, struggle, theft, or attempted theft were observed during the investigation.

Discovery of Suicide Note: Near the body, investigators discovered a handwritten note. Handwriting analysis authenticated the note as authored by Professor Mathur. In the note, Professor Mathur confessed to his participation in a black magic ritual a decade prior, resulting in the death of a young girl. He cited overwhelming guilt stemming from this event as the motive for his suicide.

Conclusion: Based on the gathered evidence, including the poison bottle, forensic analysis results, and the authenticated suicide note, the case has been conclusively determined as suicide. There is no indication of foul play.

Recommendations: Given the sensitive nature of the circumstances surrounding Professor Mathur's death, it is recommended that appropriate support services be offered to his family, friends, and colleagues. Furthermore, the findings of this investigation should be communicated with discretion to preserve the privacy and dignity of all involved parties.

Attachments:
Forensic Analysis Report
Handwriting Analysis Report
Copy of Suicide Note

Manoj skipped all other pages and directly went to the attachments to see the suicide note, which read as below:

My Dearest Loved Ones,

As I pen these words, my heart aches with the weight of unbearable remorse. I cannot continue to exist under the shadow of my sins. I can no longer bear the relentless burden of guilt that has plagued me for years, suffocating any flicker of hope or joy within me. It is with a heavy heart that I bid you farewell, for I have made the unbearable decision to end my own life.

A decade ago, my academic pursuits led me down a path that would forever haunt my conscience. In the remote village of Allookkara in Kerala, I participated in a ritual so dark, so perverse, that its memory has tormented me every waking moment since.

In the pursuit of knowledge, I became complicit in a tragedy of unspeakable proportions. A young girl, innocent and pure, became the sacrificial lamb upon the altar of our desires. I watched in horror as the thread snapped, and the sword fell, snuffing out her precious life in an instant. Yet, I remained frozen, paralyzed by fear and disbelief. The words of the priest-like figure echoed in my mind, warning of curses should we dare to halt the ritual. My silence at that moment has haunted me ever since, a constant reminder of my cowardice and complicity in her tragic fate.

For almost 10 years, I've carried this burden, this unfathomable guilt, like a millstone around my neck. No amount of therapy or medication could alleviate the torment within my soul. The guilt gnaws at my conscience, tearing away at the fabric of my sanity. It has seeped into every aspect of my existence, poisoning my relationships, my aspirations, and my very sense of self.

And now, as I face the abyss once more, I cannot bear the thought of continuing this charade. I cannot bear the thought of inflicting any more pain upon those I hold dear. I hope that in death, I may find the peace that has eluded me in life.

Please understand, my beloveds, that this final act is not one of cowardice, but of release. May you find the forgiveness and peace that has forever eluded me.

With all my love and deepest regrets,

Amit Mathur

Manoj calculated the year of the ritual as 2003, based on the mention of ' 10 years back' in the suicide note and the day of his death as, 18th June 2013. He concluded that the events mentioned in the unpublished report by Dinesh Menon and Prof. Amit Mathur are the same. He could make out that Dinesh Menon didn't publish due to the legal repercussions that this report can cause to himself.

Somehow, he felt his instinct shouting very loudly that this is somehow related to the ongoing serial killings, but unfortunately, both the concerned persons are deceased and he doesn't have any further details or clues to pursue.

The links between the journalist's findings and the Professor's death note, the ritualistic practices, and the mysterious poison remained obscured, the truth is as elusive as a shadow flitting through the night. It was like he got some answers which have created more further questions. Yet the determination within him spurred by the echoes of lost souls and demands for justice, stood firm.

Manoj was aware that this was merely the start. The road ahead was fraught with peril, yet the quest for truth, no matter how deeply it was buried, was a journey he felt compelled to undertake.

CHAPTER 6

A TRAIL OF SHADOWS

As dawn crept over the horizon, casting a soft glow on the sleepy towns of Kerala, Arjun started on a journey that would take him deep into the heart of darkness, tracing the steps of an elusive predator who had left a trail of sorrow in its wake. With each passing day, the weight of unsolved mysteries grew heavier, urging him forward on a path fraught with shadows and silence.

The first rays of the sun found him in Trivandrum, at the residence of Subhash Kumar, where tranquility masked a sinister reality. The absence of struggle whispered tales of a silent assassin, one who moved with chilling precision. Arjun moved through the rooms with a heavy heart, each artifact a silent witness to a life abruptly ending. His wife had left for his ancestral home and they had no kids. The stillness of the house seemed to hold its breath as he meticulously noted every detail, a silent prayer for the departed soul hanging in the air. He met a couple of people related to the case at the police station and had some details collected from them.

On the way back, by evening, he reached Kottayam. Due to the time crunch, he wanted to complete this procedure as soon as possible. He went to Dinesh Menon's apartment, which spoke of a mind consumed by the pursuit of truth. Papers and notes scattered about told stories of hidden secrets and whispered conspiracies. Here, Arjun felt a kinship with the silenced voice, a shared resolve to unearth the buried truths. The apartment, charged with silent whispers, seemed to urge him deeper into the mystery, a puzzle begging to be solved.

He learned that Manoj had visited the premises 2 days ago. Noting the scattered glass mirror and the wall, he understood that Manoj had found something. He just put a reminder for himself to call and catch up with Manoj to understand what's happening at his end.

The next day led him to Kochi, where Alex Matthew's dreams had been cruelly snatched away. The remnants of his passion for painting lingered in the air, a stark reminder of the vibrant life that once was. As Arjun's footsteps echoed in the apartment, he noticed scattered awards alongside photos of Kavitha and paintings memorabilia in every corner, highlighting the two main pillars of his life. He noted that unlike the general norms that define an artist, this guy seemed to have quite a selective OCD type with only some of the things kept in an organized way like the plastic carry bags which came with the groceries or the rough papers. The fading light of dusk wrapped around him as he departed, the spirit of the painter whispering in the twilight.

His next stop was in Calicut, at the home of Aparna Devi, where politics and power played their dangerous games. Here, the personal was deeply entwined with the politics each item within the residence a clue to the complex web of motives and secrets. Power whispered its dark tales, the silent machinations a backdrop to the tragedy that had unfolded.

The next day, the journey took him to the cold, digital world of Sofiya Ahmed in Tamil Nadu. Her workspace has already been started using by her replacement. At her apartment, her work desk, which reflected a blend of professional achievements and personal touches, offered no easy answers, reflecting the cunning of their adversary. He met the people connected with her and took the details from them, but didn't get any conclusive clues. The digital shadows hid their secrets well, but Arjun knew that even in this realm of codes and virtual trails, truth lingered, waiting to be uncovered.

As the week drew to a close, Arjun stood at the threshold of understanding, the disparate threads of each life weaving together into a whirlwind of motives and opportunities. The silence of the victims echoed in his heart, a constant reminder of the stakes at hand. The killer had moved through these lives like a ghost, leaving behind a trail of grief and unanswered questions.

But the journey was far from over. With each step, Arjun peeled back the layers of deceit, drawing closer to the heart of darkness. The answers he sought were hidden in the shadows, in the spaces between words and the silence of the victims. As the sun dipped below the horizon, casting long shadows across the land, Arjun knew that the coming days would bring him face to face with the abyss, challenging him to stare into its depths and confront the monster that lurked within.

The path ahead was uncertain, fraught with peril and heartache, but Arjun pressed on, driven by a resolve as unyielding as the coming dawn. The truth was out there, hidden in the darkness, and he would find it, no matter the cost. In the end, it was not just about solving a mystery; it was about justice for the silenced voices, a quest for peace in the shadow of unspeakable tragedy.

After a week of traversing the haunting landscapes of Kerala and Tamil Nadu, visiting the silent witnesses of crimes yet unsolved, Arjun returned to the heart of his operation—the place where cold facts met the burning need for justice. The team awaited; their faces etched with the fatigue of countless hours spent chasing shadows.

He settled into the familiar confines of the strategy room, a sense of urgency wrapping around him like a cloak. "We need to wrap this up soon," Arjun started, his voice carrying the weight of unmet expectations and unsolved mysteries. "Time isn't on our side, and neither is public patience. People are panicking and also scared that they might be the next victim. Plus, I have a reputation to maintain."

His team nodded, understanding the stakes. They gathered around, pouring over the scattered findings, the disparate threads of information that refused to weave into a coherent narrative. The room buzzed with the low hum of strained thoughts and whispered frustrations.

“We’re missing something,” Arjun stated, breaking the heavy silence. “There has to be a connection we’re not seeing. These people—there’s no apparent link, but there has to be. Randomness isn’t this killer’s style.”

His team exchanged looks, their expressions a mixture of doubt and determination. “We’ve combed through every detail, Arjun,” one of them replied, “but there’s nothing. No shared locations, no mutual acquaintances. It’s as if the killer is playing a game with us.”

Arjun asked,” What about the evidence collected from the locations?”

“Nothing there. All those items had been examined by us as well as the forensic team multiple times.” Maya replied in a desperate voice.

The frustration was palpable, hanging in the air like a thick fog. It was then that Arjun remembered Manoj. “I need a different perspective. I’m meeting Manoj tonight; maybe he’s seen something we haven’t.”

•••

The bar was dimly lit, the kind of place where secrets mingled freely with the smoke and the whiskey. Manoj was there, his face a mask of weariness tinged with the faintest spark of curiosity.

“As elusive as ever, Manoj,” Arjun greeted, taking the seat across from him.

Manoj managed a wry smile. “Arjun, to what do I owe the pleasure? Hoping to find the missing piece of your puzzle in the bottom of a glass?”

Arjun didn’t return the smile. “Actually, I need to talk to you about Kavitha. What have you found out?”

Manoj leaned back, his eyes narrowing slightly as he recalled his findings. “Kavitha, huh? She’s a brilliant mind, Arjun—a psycho genius, to put it bluntly. Her professors, her classmates, they all say the same. But,” he paused, his gaze locking with Arjun’s eyes, “she’s not our missing link. We looked into her, but she’s not part of this grim puzzle. We’ve abandoned that trail.”

Arjun processed the information, a part of him disappointed, yet another, more rational part, relieved. "So, she's just a brilliant mind caught in the crossfire of suspicion. No ties to the case?"

"None," Manoj confirmed, his voice firm. "She's eccentric, sure, but not criminal. Our killer is someone else, Arjun. Someone we're yet to uncover."

The conversation shifted then, to what Manoj found in Dinesh's apartment and Dr. Varma's theories. The night wore on, the clock ticking away as they delved deeper into the case, the whiskey a silent third participant in their deliberations.

As Arjun left the bar, the chill night air felt like a splash of clarity while reaching home. Arjun carefully sifted through the stack of printouts Kavitha had handed him. Each page seemed to hold a piece of the puzzle he had been trying to solve. He noted the key points, underlining some, and circling others, his mind buzzing with new ideas and connections. He read and read the relevant portion in the synopsis, which he understood that she had specially prepared for him to provide an overall picture about this concept and the technology she developed:

"This alternate universe travel is possible by utilizing a combination of cutting-edge quantum mechanics, string theory, experimental pharmacokinetics, horological engineering and neurobiology. Quantum entanglement, a phenomenon observed in particle physics, serves as the foundational principle for establishing a connection between the user and their alternate self. According to quantum physics, particles can exist in multiple states simultaneously. This theory, when extended to larger scales, suggests the existence of parallel universes where alternate versions of our reality unfold. The key lies in manipulating quantum entanglement to create a bridge between these universes. This process involves using principles of quantum entanglement to link the consciousness in one universe with a counterpart in another universe by aligning the quantum state of the brain's neural network in our universe with a

counterpart in the alternate universe. Such alignment would allow the transfer of the conscious state without physical displacement. The result is that, when you wake up in the other universe, you feel like the same person because you have the same memories and thoughts.

The key to inter-universe travel lies in a specially formulated quantum injection. The injectable solution, named Quantum Entanglement Compound (QeC), consists of a precise blend of exotic particles, bio-enhancers, and neural modulators; designed to synchronize the user's consciousness with the targeted alternate universe. The concoction is personalized based on an individual's unique quantum signature, ensuring a harmonious synchronization between the traveler's consciousness and the destination universe. The injection induces a controlled state of quantum entanglement, linking the traveler's consciousness to a counterpart in the alternate reality.

The wristwatch serves as the control center, housing the Quantum Entanglement Module. This module is responsible for establishing a stable connection between the user's consciousness and the alternate universe. The watch interfaces with the injected chemicals, regulating the entanglement process to ensure a seamless transition.

To maintain coherence during the inter-universe journey, the injected chemicals create a Temporal Resonance Field around the traveler. This field acts as a protective barrier, shielding the individual from the potential disorientation caused by the transition between alternate realities.

The amount of the injected medicine determines the destination within the multiverse. Different concentrations of the quantum injection correspond to distinct alternate universes, each with its own set of possibilities and variations. Users can fine-tune their experiences by adjusting the dosage, offering a spectrum of alternate realities to explore."

After what felt like hours of intense focus, Arjun leaned back in his chair, the papers spread out before him like a map of possibilities. With a sense of determination, he reached for his phone and dialed her number.

"Hello?" came her voice, crisp and professional.

"Hey," Arjun said, his tone a mix of excitement and anticipation. "I've gone through the printouts you gave me. There's a lot to understand here. Let's catch up."

There was a brief pause on the other end of the line, followed by a soft chuckle. "Sounds good," she replied. "How about we meet for coffee? In the morning?"

Arjun agreed, feeling a surge of energy coursing through him. This meeting promised to be more than just a casual catch-up. It was the beginning of a journey, one that would lead them deeper into the heart of the mystery they were determined to unravel.

The road ahead was still shrouded in uncertainty, but every conversation, every rejected hypothesis, brought him closer to the truth. He slipped into the bed, the darkness a familiar companion, his resolve stronger than ever. The case remained unsolved, but Arjun knew the dawn was coming, and with it, the light that would unveil the darkest of secrets.

CHAPTER 7

THE QUANTUM REVELATION

Arjun's curiosity had reached its peak by the time he met Kavita at her villa, the pages filled with complex terminologies and futuristic concepts clenched in his grip. "I tried to make sense of this, Kavita," he began, voice laced with a mixture of intrigue and confusion, "but I need you to explain it to me. For someone like me, it's still like something out of a science fiction movie. But before that, just one question, ' Why hasn't this been informed to the world? This can be a game changer and you could have reached heights of respect and money. Why is it still hidden?'"

Kavitha smiled, "You know Arjun, maybe you think I am crazy, but I believe that there are some inventions that we should understand that our world hasn't reached the maturity to receive. And I am sure, many scientists would be doing the same with their life-changing inventions. Sometimes, celebrity status or money won't weigh more against the harm this invention can bring to humanity if it falls into the wrong hands. Hope you got your answer. And so, I would request you also to promise me that you won't disclose about this to the world.".

Arjun nodded in agreement, but his facial expression clearly showing that he was still waiting for her to answer the first part of his earlier question.

Kavitha, ever the patient scientist, led Arjun to her worktable, cluttered with notes and various gadgets that seemed too advanced for the average eye. "I know it seems overwhelming, Arjun," she started, her tone was calm and reassuring, "but let me break it down for you."

She addressed the essence of their improbable venture, explaining the intricate interplay of quantum mechanics, string theory, and the broader interdisciplinary framework she had crafted.

"In essence, what we're attempting is to bridge the gap between our universe and a parallel one. Think of it as tuning into different frequencies on a radio; each frequency is a different universe."

Arjun nodded, though his brow furrowed in concentration. "And this Quantum Entanglement Compound... it's like the dial on that radio?"

"Exactly," Kavita beamed, pleased with his analogy. "The QeC synchronizes your brain's frequency with that of another 'you' in a parallel universe. The wristwatch," she continued, pointing to a sleek, metallic device, "acts as the conductor, guiding your consciousness to the right frequency, to your current universe. In simple words, we need to put an alarm in this watch, and at that time, it will give out a pulsating vibration in a specific frequency so that the medicine's effect wears off and your consciousness wakes up here"

Despite the clarity of her explanation, Arjun's expression remained dubious. "And we just... go to sleep? And wake up in another world?"

"Not just another world, Arjun, another you. You'll live out a day in the life of your parallel self. But it's not permanent. Once you wake up back here, you retain all memories from your experience in the other universe."

Arjun nodded but still had queries.

Arjun exhaled deeply, trying to grasp the reality that Kavita presented. It was a lot to take in, but the spark of adventure had already been ignited within him. "Okay, let's say I'm on board. How do we start?"

Kavita detailed the preparation and procedure, from the precise dosing of the QeC to the synchronization of the wristwatch. " It's crucial that we start with correct doses," she explained. "Different doses means waking up in different alternate universes. Through multiple experimental travels, I have finalized one universe where language won't be a barrier and the lifestyle can be easily adapted to. And I have found the correct dosage for the travel to that specific parallel universe."

Arjun's mind raced with the possibilities, the dangers, and the sheer novelty of the experience. "And death? If something goes wrong, what happens?"

"Death in the alternate universe won't affect your physical body here, but it can cause severe psychological trauma. We need to be cautious, Arjun. This isn't a game."

As the conversation progressed, Kavita sensed the time was right to introduce Arjun to the concept of alternate identities, an essential aspect of their journey. "Speaking of alternate universes, there's something personal I've discovered through my travels," Kavita began, shifting the topic towards the more personal dimension of their venture.

Arjun listened intently, his curiosity piqued "In one of the universes which we have chosen for our investigation, I lead a life starkly different from here. My alternate identity is Neeta, a newly joined intern at Mohit's family business headquarters. I come from Hyderabad, with my parents still living in India. It's a fresh start for me there, and I stay in a shared apartment."

Arjun raised his eyebrows, intrigued by the contrast. "Neeta, huh? Sounds like a complete shift from your current role."

"Yes, it is," Kavita admitted with a soft chuckle. "Neeta is very introverted and soft-spoken, but don't let that fool you. She's incredibly intelligent and committed to her work. It's fascinating to see how different circumstances shape us differently."

The discussion took a deeper dive as Kavita turned the focus towards Arjun's alternate identity, unveiling the layers of his other life with an attention to detail that captured the imagination. "As for you, Arjun, in another universe, you're Mohit. Imagine yourself in a different life in Dubai. Mohit is the spoiled child of an immensely rich NRI family. Picture a life where parties, luxury, and the company of friends and girlfriends define your days."

Arjun leaned in; his interest sharpened by the vivid imagery Kavita painted. "Mohit, huh? Sounds like he's living the dream."

Kavita nodded, continuing her narrative. "Yes, but there's more to him. Despite being seen as a party animal who loves being surrounded by people, Mohit possesses a sharp intellect. He's never been interested in work or the family business, yet his innovative ideas, once implemented by his family, have made them billions."

A pause allowed the weight of her words to sink in. "Mohit believes everything can be bought with money. He has a doctorate degree but chooses to live a life of leisure instead. His family is prominent; his father is a business tycoon, while his mother is a respected writer and philanthropist. He has an elder brother who constantly advises him, trying to guide his wayward path."

Arjun's expression reflected a mix of amusement and contemplation. "A doctor living the high life, with no care in the world except for the next big party. That's a stark contrast to my life here."

"It's the complexity and diversity of these alternate lives that fascinate me," Kavita shared, her eyes alight with enthusiasm. "Exploring these identities helps us understand the boundless possibilities of existence. Each life, each choice creates ripples across the fabric of the universe."

Arjun, now fully engrossed in the discussion, nodded slowly. "It's almost poetic, isn't it? Two lives, so vastly different, yet connected by the same soul. It makes you wonder about the 'what ifs.'"

Kavita smiled, pleased with his reflection. "Exactly. And that's why this journey is so important. Not just for solving the case, but for the personal insights we'll gain. Gaining insight into Mohit and Neeta allows us to view the world from a broader perspective. "

The evening sun dipped below the horizon as Arjun and Kavita sat in her villa, surrounded by stacks of notes and diagrams detailing their audacious plan for inter-universe travel. The weight of their impending journey hung in the air, palpable yet electrifying.

Arjun rubbed his temples, his brow furrowed in contemplation. "Kavita, I'll be honest. This all feels like we're entering into realms beyond our comprehension. Quantum mechanics, alternate realities... it's a lot to wrap my head around."

Kavita nodded empathetically; her gaze steady. "I understand, Arjun. It's a leap into the unknown, but it's also an opportunity—a chance to unravel the mysteries of existence, to explore what lies beyond the boundaries of our understanding."

Arjun, without any change in his emotion, expressed his concerns. "Kavita, all these sounds great and this plan to utilize alternate identities is bold. But how exactly do we intend to use this setup to pinpoint the culprit?"

Kavita leaned forward, her eyes locked on Arjun's, filled with a fierce determination. "Our entry into these universes under assumed identities will enable us to weave through societal layers undetected. As per my theory, Neeta will be connected to the alternate personality of Alex, who will be connected to the other victims somehow somewhere and also to the murderer. And the alternates of Neeta and Mohit, we can access locales, interact with key figures, and gather intelligence that would be impossible in our actual forms. We'll map out their interactions, histories, and uncover the connections to our anomalies. Our goal is to identify the culprit by piecing together evidence from these interactions."

Arjun sighed, leaning back in his chair, the scale of their plan dawning on him. "But what if something goes wrong? What if we get stuck in one of these alternate universes, lost without a way back?"

"We've planned meticulously, Arjun. Every step, every precaution has been taken to ensure our safety and a smooth transition. Besides, isn't the allure of discovery worth the risk?" Kavita's hand found Arjun's, her touch reassuring. "We are about to embark on a journey that pushes the boundaries of our understanding, to uncover truths that have remained hidden. This isn't just about the thrill of discovery—it's about using these insights to effect real-world applications and solve mysteries that have baffled us."

Arjun met Kavita's gaze, a flicker of uncertainty in his eyes. "I suppose so. It's just... overwhelming, you know? The enormity of what we're about to undertake."

Kavita smiled softly, her eyes alight with determination. "I know, Arjun. But remember why we're doing this—to uncover truths that have eluded us, to push the boundaries of human knowledge. And we're not alone in this. We have each other."

Arjun nodded, a sense of resolve settling over him. "You're right, Kavita. Together, we can do this. Let's take the first step into the unknown, together."

Through a daytime filled with whispers of doubt and promises of courage, Arjun and Kavita crafted their voyage into the unknown. As the shadows danced, Arjun's worries turned to wonder, his heart beating with the thrill of uncharted worlds. Side by side, they stood at the edge of tomorrow, ready to leap into a realm of new beginnings.

The familiar faded behind as Arjun, with a spark of resolve, stepped into the embrace of the night, murmuring to the stars, "Let's unravel the mysteries awaiting Mohit."

CHAPTER 8

NEW REALITIES

As the first light of dawn sneaked in through the gaps in the heavy curtains, it cast dancing shadows across the dimly lit room. Arjun sat on the edge of a plush bed in Kavitha's villa, holding a syringe filled with the glowing QeC solution. Beside him, Kavitha looked on, her face drenched in anxiety and hope, as she carefully prepared the injection.

"Sorry to ask this again and again, but are you sure this is going to work?" Arjun asked, his voice betraying a hint of doubt as he eyed the syringe.

Kavitha nodded; her confidence unshaken. "Absolutely, Arjun. This is something I have done by myself, and the theory is sound. This is a compound that will align your molecular structure to the frequency in the alternate universe. The next time you sleep, you should be able to transition smoothly."

Arjun took a deep breath as the weight of the moment settled over him. "And I'll be Mohit," he said, trying to get a grip on the surreal reality of taking another man's life, more for himself than to explain anything to Kavitha.

"Remember, your mission is to find the connection, Arjun. We need to bring back the information we need," Kavitha reminded him, her gaze locked onto his.

With another determined nod, Arjun injected the contents into his arm and lay back on the bed, letting the medicine run through his veins. The room seemed to spin slowly as he closed his eyes, and the soft pillow conformed to the shape of his head. The effect was mellow at the very first, then deepening, enveloping into a comforting darkness, urging on to another world.

When that feeling disappeared, and he opened his eyes again, Arjun was not in Kavitha's villa. He lay on a bed adorned richly, with luxurious linens and the decor quite more lavish than the previous. He sat up, looking around at the opulent surroundings that signified Mohit's home in the alternate universe. The transition had been complete; he was Arjun no more in the original universe and had stepped into the alternate reality as Mohit.

He moved towards the mirror, and his reflection baffled him as the appearance was exactly the same, but the attire, even to the posture and minute facial features, was now that of Mohit—the quintessential son known for his extravagant parties and carefree existence.

"This is it," Arjun muttered to himself, his voice now carrying the unmistakable timbre of Mohit. "Time to find out what secrets this universe holds."

Arjun checked Mohit's phone, lying on the floor near the bed. He saw that it showed Sunday, May 2022 and the time was 7:32 AM. It struck him that the timelines are different in different universes. The face was immediately recognized and the phone lock opened. He saw a lot of messages on card transactions for the previous day late in the night at some pub. Also, a message from a random number,

'Thanks for the night, it was great. Looking forward to another one.

Luv & kisses - Shruti'. It was not a surprise for Arjun as Kavitha had already briefed him about Mohit's lifestyle.

Stepping out of the room, Arjun, now Mohit, was greeted by the bustling energy of a household waking up to a new day. The servants moved with practiced efficiency, and his 'parents' were already seated at the breakfast table, their expressions filled with affection and expectation.

"Good morning," he greeted, his voice smooth and confident, the mask of Mohit firmly in place.

"Morning, Mohit. You're up early today," his father remarked with a hint of surprise in his voice.

Arjun inside Mohit flashed a smile, his eyes crinkling at the corners. "Just thought I'd start the day differently," he replied, slipping effortlessly into the role.

As they engaged in small talk, discussing plans for the day and commenting on trivial matters, Arjun marveled at the complexity of his situation. He was an outsider on the inside, a stranger to his own "family," tasked with unraveling a mystery that spanned universes. But it seemed like it was not at all a difficult task as Mohit himself was so far away from his family in respect of the attachment factor.

As breakfast progressed, Arjun took a moment to study the faces around him, finding eerie similarities that both comforted and unnerved him. Mohit's father, with his stern yet caring demeanor, was the spitting image of Arjun's grandfather in his own universe—a man of principles and immense love for his family.

The servants moved about, their faces lighting up with genuine surprise and delight as Mohit interacted with them, showing a side of himself that was both foreign and familiar. Arjun couldn't help but feel a pang of guilt at the deception, but he knew it was necessary to protect his true identity and fulfill his mission.

While sitting at the table, surrounded by people who knew him as Mohit but didn't truly know him, Arjun couldn't help but wonder how long he could keep up the charade before the truth inevitably came to light. This uncanny resemblance added a layer of surrealism to Arjun's mission, making him ponder the deep, possibly cosmic connections between these parallel worlds.

The maid, who came in to serve the food at the table, had the exact gait and mannerisms as Arjun's childhood nanny. Even her smile, warm and familiar, seemed to echo through the dimensions, reminding him of days long past. It was these small, almost imperceptible similarities that began to paint a picture of interconnected destinies.

With each interaction, Arjun gathered pieces of a puzzle that was grander and more intricate than he had anticipated. Each resemblance was a clue, and every familiar face was a reminder of the universality of human experience, spanning across universes yet rooted in the same soil of existential truth.

Arjun couldn't shake off the striking resemblance of Mohit's mother to his mother's sister in his own universe. Her mannerisms, and her gentle voice, were all reminiscent of the aunt who had been a constant presence in his childhood.

His sister-in-law, too, bore a resemblance to his childhood classmate and friend. The way she laughed, the way she spoke, it was like a reflection of the past intertwined with the present.

Even his brother, with his striking similarity to his colleague Manoj, made Arjun pause and ponder the interconnectedness of their lives. Later, as he walked through the lush garden, Arjun met the driver, whose laugh—a booming, hearty sound—mirrored that of his own universe's jovial shopkeeper. Each person Arjun encountered bore some shadow or echo of someone he knew "back home," stitching together the fabric of his two realities with a thread of shared connection. It was as if the universe was playing a grand game of mirrors, showing him glimpses of his own world in this parallel reality.

The lavish lifestyle, with its veneer of glamour and excess, was now his to navigate, a means to an end in his quest for answers. But beneath the surface, Arjun was acutely aware of the mission that drove him, the purpose that had compelled him to take this quantum leap.

As he excused himself from the breakfast table, Arjun couldn't help but feel a mix of anticipation and apprehension for what lay ahead. The alternate universe, with all its similarities and differences, was a puzzle waiting to be solved. And as Mohit, he was uniquely positioned to uncover the truth, no matter how deeply it was buried.

In this universe, Arjun found himself enveloped in the life of Mohit, surrounded by a family and a network of friends who were both familiar and alien. His parents, still figures of authority and love, but draped in different shades of personality, eyed him curiously over breakfast. Their rebellious son, who was usually detached and preoccupied with his lavish social life, was now engaging in thoughtful conversations, asking about their day with a sincerity that hadn't been there before.

The transformation didn't go unnoticed. Whispers of confusion and concern threaded through his circle of relatives who came to the house for the usual weekend lunch and the servants, all attributing Mohit's sudden change to a new phase or eccentric whim. They watched him closely, waiting for a slip-up, a return to his norm of carefree disregard. But Arjun, mindful of the delicate balance he had to maintain, navigated these interactions with a grace that belied his inner turmoil.

During a rare moment alone, his brother Vijay approached him who was the spitting image of Manoj, a hint of curiosity breaking through his usual reserve. "You've been... different lately. What's going on?"

Arjun paused, carefully choosing his words. "I've just been reflecting, I suppose—about what I want and the kind of person I want to become."

His brother nodded slowly, the lines of skepticism softening around his eyes. "Well, it's good to see. Just, don't lose yourself in the process."

Arjun's day was a carousel of faces and names, each person a thread in the fabric of Mohit's existence. There was the childhood friend who looked like one of his colleagues from the Delhi branch, always ready with a plan for adventure, who found Arjun's newfound contemplation puzzling yet intriguing. Then there was Rustom, Mohit's cousin brother & partner in crime, who eyed him warily, unsure what to make of this transformation.

"Man, you've been all Zen lately. Planning on joining a monastery or something?" his cousin joked as he had come over when Arjun was doing his research on Mohit's company.

Arjun chuckled, shaking his head. "No, just trying to see things a bit differently. There's more to life than just the next thrill, you know?"

His cousin raised an eyebrow, a smile playing on his lips. "I guess. Just don't turn into a total stranger, alright?"

As the day unfolded, Arjun met more of Mohit's world—friends who shared memories he had no part in creating, relatives who remembered moments he had never lived. Each interaction was a dance, a careful step between revealing too much and not enough, between being Mohit and remaining true to himself. It was a challenge, yes, but one that Arjun met with an earnestness that slowly began to bridge the gap between his two selves.

In this universe, Mohit was more than just a spoiled heir; he was a son, a brother, and a friend. And as Arjun navigated through his day, he began to understand the delicate threads of connection that bound Mohit to these people. He saw the potential for growth, for change, that Mohit himself had never realized. It was an enlightening experience, casting light on the shadows of his own perceptions and judgments.

During the day, he learned that the Gupta Family is far more rich and powerful than he thought. The entire family was staying together in a 7-bedroom luxurious villa in Emirates Hills, one of the most premium communities in Dubai. Everything in that villa was the epitome of luxury in every sense. Further, Arjun was astonished with the range of vehicles the family-owned which included a Bentley for Mohit's father, 2 Rolls Royce cars for Vijay & Mohit, and a couple of other cars like BMW coupes and mini coopers for the ladies of the house. He also understood that their corporate office is in a prestigious building in Downtown Dubai with the Burj Khalifa view and is completely owned by them. Learning about the guests who came to visit his parents that day, which he found by googling, revealed the level of influence the family had in Dubai and India.

By the end of his first day, Arjun had managed to avoid any major mishaps, maintaining a careful balance that kept Mohit's world intact yet noticeably altered. By around 9, he started receiving calls on his phone from different numbers, some saved and some random. He intentionally avoided the calls. And then, messages started flowing in from Mohit's friends, especially girlfriends asking him where he is hanging out tonight. He didn't want to take a chance and ignored all those. The maid informed him that the driver had arrived and the car was ready. But he asked the driver to leave as he was planning to stay home that night.

His uncharacteristic decision to stay in for the night instead of going out to party as Mohit typically would, raised eyebrows among the family. Even more surprising was his avoidance of the usual bickering or confrontations, which were a common end to Mohit's evenings.

He went to bed that night not in the familiar comfort of his own room, but under a sky of different stars, his mind busy pondering the lessons of identity and connection. This journey, he realized, was not just about exploring the physics of the universe but also the intricate dynamics of human relationships. The day's experiences had profoundly impacted him, introducing depth to his understanding of Mohit's life and the delicate fabric that held it together.

As he drifted off to sleep, Arjun was filled with a profound sense of curiosity and anticipation for what the next day would bring in this alternate reality, wondering how these subtle changes he introduced might ripple through the days ahead.

A pulsating feeling emerged from his hand, spreading throughout his body, and jolting him awake. It was the pulse alarm from the watch Kavitha had given him. He realized he was lying on the same bed in Kavitha's villa where he had slept the previous day.

Opening his eyes, he saw Kavitha sitting on the nearby sofa, looking at him. He could sense the triumphant emotion in her eyes.

“Welcome to your own universe,” Kavitha said, smiling.

He simply smiled back, lost in the afterglow of the extraordinary experience he had just had. Rising, he washed his face and got ready to leave. “That was... something quite different. As you said, the world around me was totally different there. Anyway, the first day was okay. Now, I think we need to catch up there and proceed with what we need to do together. So, I assume we will do the next trip tonight. Now let me do some work in this universe also.”

“Sure, Arjun,” Kavitha replied. “So, see you tonight. Let’s make sure to start early so that the day there starts early.”

Arjun reached his apartment, got ready, and headed to the station. His mind was busy working out various strategies on how to proceed in the alternate universe. The honking of a car from behind snapped him out of his thoughts, reminding him to focus on the case in this universe as well. By the time he reached the station, he had formulated some plans on how to move forward.

He called up his team, Maya and Rajiv. “I know we’ve been working towards finding the murderer by connecting the victims. Let’s take a different route, parallelly. Let’s try to find the murderer directly,” he suggested. “Maya, you go to all the crime sites and try to gather all the available footage from surveillance or security cameras in the nearby shops, roads, and houses of each site. Then coordinate with our tech team to run the facial cross matching program on all the footage to find a common face in the captures from all the locations.”

“And Rajiv, you go through similar case files from all over India to see if you find any patterns of serial killings in the same method—solved or unsolved, along with the details. Maybe our killer has struck before or is using some past killer’s strategy.”

“So, let’s move forward.”

Both Maya and Rajiv agreed and started immediately, with renewed vigor and energy.

The conference room was simple and practical, featuring a long table surrounded by comfortable chairs. Maps and boards filled with photos and notes from active cases lined the walls, and bright overhead lights cast a clear glow on the documents and coffee cups scattered across the table. A projector and screen stood ready for presentations, making it obvious that this space was used for important meetings and planning sessions. The overall atmosphere was focused and busy, reflecting the serious work that took place here.

After Rajiv and Maya left, Arjun was standing there and gazing at the board where the photos of the victims in the respective locations of their murders were fixed on a map which was looking like a big puzzle to be solved. Arjun's mind was doing calculations and working out various strategies on how to move forward in both universes parallelly and how & where to intersect them.

Suddenly, DIG Pankaj stepped into the room, his gaze scanning the walls before settling on Arjun, who was standing near the projector. "Arjun," he called out, "Tell me that you have made some progress. It has been almost a week and I expect some breakthrough on this case from you."

Arjun suddenly woke up from his train of thoughts and thought for a moment on what to answer. His inside was fighting if he should disclose the extraordinary path he has chosen to solve this case, but like an agreement to Kavitha's reservations, he chose not to tell DIG about that.

He looked at DIG whose expression was insisting on an answer.

After a couple of seconds, Arjun replied with a blank face, "Sorry to inform you that there has not been any breakthrough from my side. I promise you that I will come back to you with something very shortly." After a pause, he continued," But the good news is that Manoj was able to get some solid clues from one of the murder locations. And I am sure that we will have a door opened in front of us to go in and solve this puzzle.``

DIG, expressing the discontent on his face and tone, asked him to speed up and close the case on a war footing basis. And he left the room, closing the door behind.

Arjun, with a deep breath, took out the forensic reports of all the murders and started going through the same, aiming to find something that might have missed out. While going through the summary report by Manoj's team, his thoughts got stuck on something. He called a constable and asked to get the box containing the items connected to these serial killings from the evidence room. He patiently waited and as soon as the box was kept on the conference room table, he started checking inside it frantically for something specific. Unable to find what he was looking for, he took the phone and called Maya.

"Yes Sir, I am on the way to Trivandrum. Anything I can help you with?"

"Maya, just one question. Did you guys get hold of the envelope in which the canvas was sent to Alex Mathew? I am not able to find that in the evidence box."

Maya, after a small pause, replied "I don't remember collecting that. No, I am sure. There was no envelope collected."

"Thanks, Maya." He disconnected the phone, kept the reports on the table and rushed out.

After driving for some time, he reached in-front of a residential building in which there was the apartment of Alex Mathew. He entered the apartment with the spare key from the police department and started combing the room. After a deep search inside the nook and corner of the apartment, he found an envelope neatly bent and kept among the carry bags and other such stuff below his work table. After wearing a new set of gloves, he took it out and opened it slowly. It seemed to be a big one that was used to cover a big canvas. It had some paint on the inside shouting that it was used to cover the canvas immediately after it was painted, making it clear that the canvas from the murderer came as a courier in this envelope. On a brief investigation of the same, he found nothing unusual.

He took it with him and drove back to the station. As soon as he reached, he went to the forensic team and asked them to investigate it very carefully. They started working on that while Arjun sat waiting in his office impatiently. He was eagerly expecting some breakthrough from this new finding.

CHAPTER 9

SHADOWED PATHS

The rain hammered relentlessly against the windows of the forensic lab, a somber backdrop to the groundbreaking revelations unfolding within its walls. Manoj stood in the muted light, a sheaf of papers in his hand, each sheet a testament to the blend of science and sleuthing that had brought him to this pivotal moment. The latest update from the lab was a breakthrough in the case: traces of poison in the marijuana, a concoction so rare it unmistakably linked all the serial killings to a meticulous and singularly cunning mind.

"Congratulations Manoj, this is a great breakthrough in this case, you know. To date, it was just an assumption on the poison part but now we have the evidence. And while I did a simulation by adding this poison to blood, it changed the composure of the blood to a form that was similar to the blood samples from all the victims in this serial killing case. The chemical composition," Dr. Varma continued explaining, "isn't something you stumble upon by accident. It's deliberate, crafted. Whoever did this had access to some pretty obscure knowledge, likely sourced from the darker corners of the internet."

Recognizing the significance of this discovery, Manoj immediately instructed the police force to inform the pharmacist network, instructing them to keep an eye out for anyone attempting to purchase this unique combination of chemicals. This new strategy soon bore fruit, as information began trickling in from various pharmacists. However, despite these promising tips, none provided a solid lead.

The investigation, though invigorated by this major development, still faced the challenge of pinpointing the elusive murderer.

Manoj's mind raced, connecting dots in a pattern that remained frustratingly incomplete. "And you're certain there's no trace of these chemicals being purchased under the radar? No unusual orders or inquiries that might lead us to a supplier?" he pressed, clinging to the hope of a lead.

"Nothing. I checked through my sources also. It's like they've vanished into thin air," Dr. Varma replied, a note of frustration in his voice.

With a determined nod, Manoj tucked the report under his arm, stepping out into the rain-drenched noon. His next stop was the underbelly of the city, where whispers and shadows intertwined in a tenuous dance.

His network of informers, a ragtag group bound by necessity rather than loyalty, had been his eyes and ears on the street. Today, he hoped they would be his guide through the murk of uncertainty.

The informant's den was a nondescript building in Fort Kochi, its façade weathered by time and neglect. On the frontside, it was an antique shop but deep inside the shop, there was a secret door which opened into a big hall-like area, that was completely a different world, or rather an underworld. The area was well guarded but no one stopped Manoj from entering as they knew his aggressive attitude, if provoked. Inside, amid the haze of cigarette smoke and the low murmur of conversation, Manoj found his contact, a man known only as Ravi, nursing a glass of tea that had long since gone cold.

"Sir, I told you earlier also, there is no talk about any contracts for any of these murders. But, about Dinesh's contacts with drug peddlers, it's true. He is a regular customer. And he regularly buys it from a guy named Jayesh. But all the arrangements are handled by Dinesh's manager only". Ravi began without preamble, his gaze fixed on a spot somewhere beyond the walls of the room. "But the word is, your guy was expecting a delivery. But by the time the carrier reached there, he saw someone leaving on a bike and on enquiring, the manager informed him that the delivery was accepted assuming that it was Jayesh's guy only. Thought it was odd."

"So, it was a delivery that was intercepted?" Manoj mused aloud, the pieces of the puzzle shifting, forming a new image.

"Could be, but there's talk of a new player, someone not known to the usual circles," Ravi added, lowering his voice.

The mention of a new player ignited a flicker of hope in Manoj's relentless pursuit. He took Ravi along with him and went to meet Jayesh. On questioning Jayesh, Manoj understood that the new player was just an imaginary one, based on this intercepted delivery and Jayesh's network had no further clue about that. He asked deeper questions, probing until it surfaced that there was a helper, Dinesh Menon's manager Asif, who facilitated these clandestine exchanges and had taken this delivery from this so-called 'new player's' carrier. Manoj, without wasting any further time, started off to Kottayam to meet Asif once again.

Asif, a young man caught in a web of circumstance and desperation, was more forthcoming under the weight of Manoj's scrutiny. "I don't know much, sir," he stammered, a bead of sweat tracing a path down his forehead. "Just that there was someone new last time. A guy, who was wearing a helmet. Didn't say much. Just that - He is here to do the delivery"

"A helmet..." Manoj repeated, the detail etching itself into his memory. "No name, no distinguishing feature?"

Asif nodded in disagreement and then suddenly, like he woke up from a dream, "Just that the guy had green-colored eyes".

Manoj noted that point in his mind and asked again, "That's good, and nothing else?"

Asif shook his head, his eyes wide with the fear of remembrance. After questioning him for some more time, Manoj understood that there was nothing more left to be extracted. He warned Asif not to go out of the city till further notice and left the place.

On the way back to Kochi from Kottayam, Manoj was trying to put the pieces of the puzzle together with whatever he had found, but he understood that there were still a lot of missing pieces and it seemed like he needed to get the pieces found by Arjun also, to try and solve it. Despite knowing it was late and well past Arjun's usual bedtime, he dialed Arjun's number. After a few rings, Arjun picked up and said, "Hey Manoj, where have you been? It's like you vanished for an entire day!"

"I was following a trail, Arjun, which took me to Kottayam. Now I am on my way back to Kochi and will reach within 15-20 minutes. I think we need to bring our parallel investigations a bit closer and try to fill the gaps with each other's findings. Where are you now? Can we catch up?"

"Sorry Manoj, I don't think I will be able to make it today. I am at Kavitha's villa and we have some work to complete, or rather start with. Let's meet tomorrow. what say?"

"Cool Arjun. Will connect tomorrow then. Bye good night."

Even though Manoj responded casually, his mind was trying to find answers to this close connection that developed between Arjun and Kavitha in a span of just a week. Being buddies, Manoj decided to ask Arjun openly about this during his next meeting.

Once again, Manoj went back to his mental calculations analysing the findings till date.

CHAPTER 10

PURSUIT ACROSS REALMS

Meanwhile, in the grandeur that marked the Gupta Regal Group's headquarters, a building that pierced the sky with its imposing presence, Arjun paced the length of Mohit's luxurious office, his thoughts a tempest. Since stepping into this alternate universe and assuming Mohit's identity, every moment felt like a walk on a tightrope. But today, the second day of visit, was different; today, he had a purpose that quickened his heartbeat—a meeting with his assistant, whom he believed to be Kavitha's alternate self.

The intercom buzzed, slicing through his contemplations. "Sir, Ms. Neeta is in," announced the receptionist who was told to inform him as soon as Neeta entered the building.

"Send her into my office" Mohit responded, his voice steady despite the storm of emotions within him.

The door opened, and she stepped into the room—a mirror image of Kavitha, yet not quite her. As their eyes met, a silent acknowledgment passed between them. The connection was instant, a thread woven from the fabric of their shared quest across universes.

Neeta's gaze was quizzical, feigning ignorance as she looked Arjun over. "I'm sorry for being late, Mr. Mohit," she said with a perfectly crafted note of confusion in her voice.

Arjun, still in the guise of Mohit, felt a jolt of confusion. His mind raced as he tried to grasp the situation, the familiarity of her features stark against her feigned unfamiliarity.

As they sat, the guise of formalities slowly melted away, but Neeta maintained her act, replacing expected pleasantries with puzzling statements. "I'll be sure not to repeat myself coming late next time," she continued with a mischievous glint in her eye.

The moment stretched, Arjun's confusion deepening. Just as he began to question the very basis of their meeting, Kavitha burst into laughter from where she stood.

"It's just a joke, Arjun!" Kavitha exclaimed, stepping into view with a playful smirk.

"Kavitha, you're the worst!"

Relief washed over Arjun, replaced quickly by amusement as he realized the extent of their playful deception. This lighthearted interlude, orchestrated by Kavitha, highlighted her youthful, spirited nature, showcasing a rare glimpse into her less-serious side amidst the gravity of their mission.

Suddenly, Neeta's phone buzzed on the table, its sharp hum cutting through their conversation. The screen lit up with a name: '**Psycho Brother**'. Without a word, she reached out, pressed the side button, and the buzzing stopped. The room seemed to hold its breath for a moment.

Kavitha's laughter faded into a more serious tone as she observed Arjun's reaction. "But let's not lose focus, Arjun," she said, her voice firm yet still carrying a hint of levity. "We have a complex task ahead, and every bit of information is crucial. You've been here a day longer; what have you gathered?"

Arjun glanced at Kavitha, his expression darkening slightly. "I've been trying to piece together the network here," Arjun whispered, leaning closer. "The dynamics are different, yet some things feel hauntingly similar."

Neeta's phone buzzed again, the screen lighting up with the same name: '**Psycho Brother**.'

"Aren't you going to answer that?" Arjun asked, glancing at the phone.

Neeta shook her head firmly. "I can't," she said, her voice low. "If he doubts the way I'm talking or senses anything off in my behavior, he might suspect something."

"You should still answer it," Arjun insisted.

"No," she repeated, more firmly this time. "I can't risk it. That's too close."

The phone buzzed a third time before falling silent. Neeta let out a breath she didn't know she'd been holding. "He's relentless. But as long as I don't give him anything, he won't have a reason to be suspicious."

Arjun nodded thoughtfully. "Okay, just be careful. We can't afford to slip up now."

Neeta flashed him a reassuring smile. "Don't worry. I've got this."

Arjun returned her smile, appreciating her confidence. "All right. Let's continue."

With the playful energy behind them, they leaned into their planning, reviewing every information and clues they had gathered from their own universe, while both of them taking notes and interjecting each other with their observations on how to utilize those in this universe.

The atmosphere turned tense as they diligently worked to untangle the web of mysteries standing between them and the truth. Little did they realize, however, that the '**Psycho Brother**,' whose calls they were deliberately ignoring, would soon become a pivotal milestone and a significant step towards the success of their investigative journey.

After a while, Arjun got into deep thinking, while his eyes scanning the opulent office, a stark contrast to their purpose

He asked, "I've noticed that this universe has its own version of the puzzle we're trying to solve. During your previous journeys to here, have you found anything on Alex or any of the characters?"

"Not yet. But with you here, we have a better chance. We need to tread carefully, though. Remember, we're not just fighting a hidden enemy; we're navigating a world that's not our own," Kavitha cautioned, the weight of their double lives bearing down on her.

Arjun nodded in agreement.

"Ok now, see Arjun, the photos of the victims won't be necessary," Kavitha interjected, her mind racing with possibilities. "I can capture the likenesses of the victims and that of Prof. Amit Mathur, by memorizing the photos you shared with me. My sketches should suffice for cross-referencing with the alternate personalities of the victims in this universe. But even without a wide search, we should be able to find Alex's alternate personality as that person will be connected to me, I mean Neeta, closely in this universe. As Alex's influence extends here, we might find our first lead easily."

Arjun's gaze settled on her, admiration and gratitude mingling in his look. "Your ability to adapt and use your skills creatively, even in a place as overwhelming as this, is what's going to get us through."

Their conversation once again shifted to strategies and next steps, a dance of words and plans that spanned realms and dangers. As the meeting drew close, Arjun and Kavitha knew their path was fraught with uncertainties. Yet, the resolve that had brought them together across universes burned brighter than ever.

"Let's meet again after you've completed creating the sketches. We'll need to start with our actions immediately," Arjun suggested as they stood.

"Agreed. And thank you, Mr. Mohit, for this opportunity," Kavitha said, her voice a blend of formality and secret solidarity as she felt a presence at the door.

As Kavitha left the office, Arjun watched her go, a sense of camaraderie and purpose reinforcing the bond they shared. In the heart of the Gupta Regal Group, amid the trappings of wealth and power, a battle for truth and justice was quietly taking shape, led by two souls united by a cause greater than themselves.

Arjun turned back to the panoramic view of the Burj Khalifa from his office, a symbolic lookout point for the challenges ahead. With Kavitha by his side, even in disguise, he felt a surge of optimism. Together, they would unravel the mysteries of this universe, one clue at a time.

Just then, a thought struck him, and he rushed out of the office. He needed to find out if his girlfriend, Divya, existed in this universe. He was expecting to find her here, as she was also in Dubai in 2022 and that's the year currently running in this universe for him. Beyond the desire to see her and understand who she was in this reality, he also hoped to leverage her network to track down the alternate versions of those involved in the case.

Taking Mohit's car, he drove straight to Bank Street in Bur Dubai, heading for the building where Divya's office was supposed to be. As he frequently visited her while in his own universe, the roads were familiar, just as they did in his own universe. Upon arrival, he approached the reception and inquired about her company. But to his surprise, no such company existed. Refusing to accept this, he went up to the third floor—where her office should have been—only to find a completely different setup, occupied by multiple unrelated businesses.

Determined, he searched for her company name on Mohit's phone, but nothing came up. Clinging to hope, he rushed to the location where her villa should have been—only to find that it didn't exist here either.

Disheartened, he drove back to the office, his mind replaying what Kavitha had said—alternate personalities in different universes could be leading entirely different lives. With a wry smile, he realized the futility of his search and chuckled at his own naive expectations.

Just then he received a call from Kavitha asking where he was. She had completed creating the sketches and wanted to meet him. It was approaching mid noon in the alternate universe, the air was charged with a sense of urgency, yet the city around him pulsed with the mundane rhythm of daily life, oblivious to the inter-universal travelers in its midst. He increased the speed of the car.

As soon as he reached Mohit's office, Kavitha came in. She handed over the papers where she had brought the images of the victims to life. "And these," she said, gesturing to her drawings, "will help us jog memories, stir recognition. It's our best shot at finding someone who's seen them."

Arjun nodded his head in agreement.

Their first task was clear: finding the alternate personalities of all the victims and among those, they assumed that the easiest to find should be that of Kavitha's boyfriend, Alex, a pivotal figure in the puzzle they were desperate to solve. Arjun, with his access to Mohit's considerable resources, planned to immediately set to work, leveraging his influence and financial power to gather information.

"Finding Alex can be a key," Arjun asserted, scanning the network of contacts on Neeta's phone, iPad, and laptop. They learned that she was not a heavy social media user also – she only seemed to be active in Linkedin. And hence in Facebook or Instagram, there were only couple of friends and almost no pictures to check for connections through photos uploaded. According to Kavitha's theory, Alex's alternate personality should be closely connected to Neeta in this universe. "We can expect that others would be connected to Alex's alternate personality somehow. So, once we find him and understand his connection to the other victims, we can start unraveling the mystery from there."

Before Kavitha could respond, Neeta's phone buzzed on the table. The screen lit up with the name: '**Psycho Brother**'. Once again, she silenced the device.

She winked at him with a naughty smile, gesturing that it was being taken care of.

Kavitha, still in Neeta's disguise, took a deep breath and faced Arjun with a devilish smile. "Arjun," she began, her voice steady and confident, "I've arranged for a surprise meeting with someone very close to you. This person, once convinced, can be crucial in helping us find the people we're looking for."

Arjun's eyes widened slightly, curiosity and hope flickering across his face. "Who is it?" he asked, his tone eager yet cautious.

Kavitha blinked and smiled mysteriously. "You'll see soon enough. Trust me, this meeting could change everything. And make sure to take the photos of the victims in your phone and keep it always with you"

Arjun nodded, the anticipation building within him. He knew that every step they took brought them closer to the truth, and with Kavitha by his side, he felt more prepared than ever to face whatever challenges lay ahead.

Arjun sat shocked right across from Shafna in a dimly lit café, the gentle hum of conversation filling the space around them. Shafna Ali was one of Mohit's occasional companions, someone he'd met at a late-night party. Shafna worked in the IT department of the Dubai Police and occasionally helped Mohit with information that wasn't easily accessible.

As Arjun looked at her, a wave of emotions surged through him. He felt a jolt of recognition, his heart aching with the memory of Divya. The resemblance was uncanny, almost painful. It had been so long since he'd seen her face, and the flood of memories and emotions was almost overwhelming. For a brief moment, he allowed himself to feel the joy of reunion, the warmth of familiarity.

But as the seconds ticked by, reality set in. This was not Divya; this was Shafna, her alternate personality in this universe. The complexity of their situation weighed heavily on him. How could he navigate this intricate web of alternate identities and relationships?

The lines between his past and present, between different versions of people he once knew, were blurred and tangled. He thought about the immense challenge of their mission, and the emotional toll of seeing familiar faces in unfamiliar roles.

The shock of the initial encounter began to settle, replaced by a determined resolve. He needed to stay focused, to use the connection with Shafna to their advantage. Despite the emotional whirlwind, Arjun knew that every interaction, every piece of information, brought them one step closer to unraveling the truth.

Kavitha had planned this meeting meticulously, knowing that Shafna could be instrumental in their search for the murder victims. As they settled into their chairs, Arjun began, his voice steady, "We're investigating something. We believe the people in these drawings," he said, nodding towards Kavitha's sketches laid out on the table, "are connected to a series of... events that need to be addressed. Have you seen any of them? And can you please help me with finding these people using your access to the system and resources"

Shafna, initially skeptical, studied the faces before her. Then, like something else struck her mind, she looked up and with a smile spoke, "Mohit, it's a surprise to see you requesting something. Usually, you call and just order. Seems you are quite different when sober and I'm loving that". And she kissed him on his cheek.

Arjun smiled while nodding in agreement, hiding the fear inside.

Shafna continued, "And about finding these people, Yeah, I can try. See, I can comb the system files and if any of these people were involved in any cases or accidents, I will be able to find them. This can be done from my system at home. You want to do it now?"

Arjun agreed, and they set off for her apartment in Business Bay, which was located near the café where they had been sitting.

When they arrived at her door, Shafna moved swiftly, unlocking it in one fluid motion and ushering him inside. The apartment was warmly lit, with an understated elegance—soft beige tones on the walls, a hint of lavender lingering in the air. The door had barely clicked shut when Shafna turned to Arjun, her expression a mix of urgency and vulnerability.

Before he could process her intent, she closed the space between them, her arms wrapping tightly around his shoulders. Her embrace was both frantic and tender, as though she were holding onto something fleeting. Her lips found his, their softness igniting a spark that melted the restraint in him. The kiss deepened, unspoken emotions unfurling in its intensity, her fingertips brushing the back of his neck as though anchoring herself to him.

Arjun hesitated for the briefest moment, a sliver of doubt flashing in his mind. But his mind convinced him with the justification that this was Divya only, and if this was Divya, was it not right to give in, to reciprocate what she so desperately sought?

What followed was a storm of passion—unrestrained, fervent, and fleeting. The air between them crackled with an unspoken understanding as they surrendered to the moment.

After that, while lying in the bed together, Shafna asked, "How long has it been Mohit, since we had such a catch-up after that New Year party night? And you know Mohit, you are so soft when sober, in talks as well as actions" and she laughed at her own joke. Noticing that Mohit had become serious, she stood up, still covered by a silky bed sheet, sat in front of her desktop with an enormous sized screen, and connected her work Macbook to it. She navigated the system like a seasoned pro, and soon, they identified the first two victims from an accident report by their vehicle registration details.

Shafna started, "They were involved in an accident near the marina; two cars collided, but nothing fatal. I can download the accident report along with their driving license copies if you want."

Arjun leaned back, a smile forming on his lips. "That would be incredibly helpful."

She opened the accident report and their driving licenses in the system monitor for them to view and meanwhile put instructions for printing out the files. One was Ala Mohammad, from Egypt and the other was Manish Singh, an Indian expat. Arjun checked the photos and recognized them as the alternate personalities of Subhash Kumar and Dinesh Menon, respectively. He was quite surprised and happy with this breakthrough on the second day itself.

Arjun asked, "Anything on the other 4 faces?"

"Nothing in the existing files, But I can put their faces in the system," Shafna said, "but I can only use the active search mode. It's not an officially approved investigation, so the system will only alert me when any of them come in front of one of the cameras. But with Dubai police having cameras every nook and corner, I think we will get the hit within no time."

"Understood," Arjun nodded. "Please do it for me?" he asked, pointing at Kavitha's sketches.

Shafna agreed. "I'll put all four photos in the system and update you once any of them are found. But be aware that this could take time."

Arjun thanked her, and Shafna assured him she would keep him updated. With that, they both left the apartment—Shafna returning to the police station and Arjun heading to his office.

Back in the office, Kavitha waited patiently, reviewing notes and organizing the information they had gathered so far. When Arjun returned, she looked up expectantly. "How did it go?"

"Shafna is on board," Arjun replied, showing excitement. "We have got the details of two of them and She's put all the other 4 faces in the system and will alert us once any of them show up on the camera network."

"Wow, that's a great breakthrough!" Kavitha said, relieved. "That should help us get closer to the victims just like you and Divya in this universe too."

Ignoring the sarcastic quote, Arjun leaned against the desk, folding his arms thoughtfully. "I've been thinking about Mohit's family. I feel like I should try to reconnect them with each other. Maybe I can do something to help somehow."

Kavitha's expression hardened. "Don't ever do such things, Arjun. It will cause a big ripple effect in the cosmic balance and disrupt Mohit and his family's lives. Let him fight his own war."

Arjun sighed but nodded in agreement. "You're right. I just thought maybe..."

"Maybe you could make things better?" Kavitha interjected gently. "I understand, but meddling with their lives would only complicate things further. We have to stay focused on our mission."

Arjun nodded again. "All right. Let's concentrate on finding these people."

Without wasting time, Arjun and Kavitha rushed to find those two individuals using the address details they got from Shafna. However, when they finally met with them, they didn't yield any helpful clues. The two individuals seemed genuinely perplexed, unsure of what information Arjun and Kavitha were trying to obtain.

At that point of time, both of them realized that finding the people was only a start and they needed to find a way to understand the commonly connected persons with all of them, but without disclosing about all these 'alternate universe concepts. '

Both of them were brainstorming on how to move forward while getting ready to travel back to their own universes, as it was going to be night.

They slept at their respective homes and within no time, Arjun and Kavitha woke up in their own universe, their minds clouded with confusion and uncertainty. The air was thick with an unfamiliar tension, and their surroundings seemed distorted, almost like a dream.

Arjun checked his phone and noticed several missed calls from the DIG. "Looks like I have got work to do. Let's catch up and analyze today evening before we make the travel tonight" he said to Kavitha. He quickly returned the call and was summoned to the DIG's office.

Arjun dialed Rajiv's number and waited as the phone rang. After a few moments, Rajiv answered, his voice slightly muffled. "Hey Arjun, what's up?"

"Hey Rajiv, come over for a catch-up meeting. Manoj and I are going to the DIG's office and we need to have an update meeting there. Call Maya, and ask her also to reach there," Arjun replied, a sense of urgency creeping into his voice.

"Sure, I'll be there in a bit," Rajiv replied before ending the call.

After around an hour, Rajiv and Maya arrived at DIG's office, greeted by Arjun and Manoj. They quickly got down to business, and Arjun filled Rajiv & Maya in on the latest developments in the case while waiting to meet the DIG. After a couple of minutes, they were called in and Arjun went in to meet the DIG along with Manoj. Rajiv and Maya waited in the outside office room eagerly.

At the DIG's office, Arjun stood before the desk, his posture firm. The DIG eyed him intently. "Good morning, Arjun and Manoj. Manoj, it's good to see you tagging along. Arjun, we've been trying to reach you. What's the update on your initiatives?"

Arjun cleared his throat and responded, "Sir, Manoj and I have been investigating separately but it seems we need to pursue both paths parallelly but together, to speed up the process. We've instructed Rajiv and Maya on gathering intelligence and we will be working on the results today. However, it appears we're dealing with an elusive presence. We're finding patterns, but no solid leads."

After providing their updates, Arjun and Manoj met up with Rajiv and Maya in Arjun's office.

Arjun turned to Rajiv. "Rajiv, I had asked you to look into any similar serial killings across India. Did you find anything?"

Rajiv listened intently and then shook his head. “No serial killings in this format anywhere in India in recent times.”

Arjun turned to Maya, his expression expectant as if anticipating good news from her. The atmosphere grew increasingly tense as Maya began her briefing.

“So far, we have no solid findings based on your assignment,” Maya said, laying out sketches and notes on the table. “The software couldn’t find any common faces at all locations, but there’s one consistent presence—a person wearing a hoodie with ‘Fallen Angel’ printed on its back. Unfortunately, we can’t see the face, and we can’t determine if it’s a he or she.”

Arjun and Manoj exchanged a concerned glance. “This person,” Arjun mused, “appears everywhere but remains invisible.”

“It’s like they’ve all been touched by the same darkness,” Manoj muttered as he glanced at one of the captured pictures. “We need to find out who stands at the center of this web.”

Arjun leaned back, his mind racing. “Let’s think about their stories, their encounters. The commonality is stark, and yet the connections are thin.”

The threads of the investigation were quite blurred, hinting at a complexity of lives crossed and marked by a hidden hand. As they digested this reality, the mystery deepened, pulling them further into the shadows of this tangled reality.

CHAPTER 11

REGENERATED REFLECTIONS

Manoj was driving back to his station after the catchup meeting, and on the way, he received a call from the IT team with the update that the photos, he had found at Dinesh Menon's apartment, had been reconstructed. Manoj immediately called Arjun, requesting him to meet him at the lab. He involuntarily increased the speed of his Jeep replicating the excitement and his eagerness to know about the clues waiting for them among those reconstructed photos.

•••

By the time Manoj reached the lab, Arjun was already there. At the Lab, Arjun and Manoj huddled around the computer screen in the dimly lit lab, their eyes fixed on the images displayed before them. The room was filled with a tense silence as they studied the faces of the victims, each one a tragic reminder of lives cut short.

"These images are more than just victims; they're pieces of a puzzle," Manoj murmured, his voice laced with determination. He carefully traced the contours of each face, searching for a connection that would unravel the mystery before them.

The tech team had made significant progress, managing to regenerate the photos recovered along with the report from Dinesh Menon's secret locker. They had developed images of four faces separately, with remarkable clarity: 3 of them looked like they were in their 20's & one was a bit older, of about 30-35. However, their efforts were thwarted when it came to the remaining two faces, as they were partially obscured by fire and shadows. The other two faces remained elusive, shrouded in mystery.

Arjun and Manoj examined the photos closely, their brows furrowed in concentration. None of the four faces seemed immediately familiar, but something about one of the images caught Manoj's attention. He pulled out his phone and opened the photo of Prof. Amit Mathur, leaning in to compare it closely with that specific reconstructed image. Despite the passage of time, the features of the faces remained eerily similar, hinting at a connection that transcended the confines of the digital realm.

"Arjun, look at this," Manoj said, pointing to the photos. "Don't both resemble each other?"

Arjun scrutinized the images before nodding slowly. "You're right. It's uncanny. There has to be a link."

The realization sent a chill down their spines. They rechecked trying to match any other photos with that of the victims and they saw a similar resemblance to another reconstructed image to the photo of Aparna Devi also. The ritual seemed to have ties to the serial killing case they had been working on. But they wanted to reconfirm it and for that, they needed to dig deeper.

"What if we use the aging algorithm on all the regenerated photos?" Arjun suggested. "Maybe we'll uncover new leads, new connections."

Manoj nodded, his mind racing ahead to the possibilities. "It's worth a shot. Let's get the tech team on it right away."

The tech team assembled in the conference room, their laptops glowing with data streams and photo-enhancing software. They listened intently as Arjun and Manoj explained the new task.

"We need you to age all these photos by 20 years using AI technology," Manoj instructed. "Let's see what connections we can uncover."

"Understood, sir," one of the tech specialists replied. "It will take some time, but we'll get it done."

Before dispersing, another technician approached, holding a photograph of a young girl on an altar. "We found this also among the files," she said, handing the picture to Manoj. "Do we need to work on this too?"

Manoj studied the photo, the girl's face frozen in a timeless moment of ritual and mystery. "I am not sure if that will be of any use. But let's see if she will tell us some story. "Make sure she's also included."

The tech team nodded in agreement, and the room buzzed with renewed determination. With the new directive, the investigation had entered a critical phase. The aging algorithm could be the key to unlocking connections hidden beneath layers of time. As the tech team got to work, Arjun and Manoj exchanged a look of understanding. They both knew that what they were going to uncover in the coming days could be crucial in solving the case, but it would require every ounce of their focus and skill.

After some moments, Manoj, who was still staring at the screen with the girl's photo on it mentioned, "Well, there might be something else also worth looking into. Dinesh Menon's report mentions Allookkara as the location where the ritual took place. If the incident mentioned in that report, the faces in these photos and the serial killings are connected, we might be able to find some leads there. Maybe some relatives or a lover can provide valuable insights."

Arjun and Manoj exchanged a glance, the pieces of the puzzle slowly falling into place.

"That could be a new lead," Manoj said, his voice filled with determination. "I think this lead should be pursued and see what we can find."

Arjun made a call to Rajiv. "Hey Rajiv, I am sending you the regenerated picture of the girl, who is assumed to be killed during the ritual mentioned in Dinesh Menon's report. Using this photo, I need you to go to Allookkara and do a detailed inquiry into this occurrence mentioned in the report. See if there are any relatives of that girl or any old lovers. Also, assist Manoj with whatever he needs."

Armed with this new information, Rajiv set out to Allookkara, his mind buzzing with possibilities.

As the team delved deeper into the investigation, they knew they were one step closer to unraveling the truth behind these heinous crimes.

CHAPTER 12

HUNTERS GAME

Arjun's routine had shifted significantly over the past few days. He now slept at Kavitha's villa every day, as it would make the journey to the alternate universe easier and give them some time together in the evenings to catch up and discuss the steps to be taken during each day's journey. In the morning, once they wake up here, he will rush to his hotel room to get ready and work on the investigation in this universe. And Kavitha will spend her days consumed in her research, revising her work based on her travel experiences, and analyzing the information collected during her previous trips. They both traversed the thin veil between realities, becoming accustomed to the peculiarities of this strange, dual life. Their evenings passed amid caffeine and strategic planning.

Arjun known for his relentless pursuit of justice, found himself under an unexpected spotlight. Assigned to a high-profile case, his every move was now a matter of public scrutiny. The media followed him like a shadow, eager to capture any hint of scandal or intrigue.

On the third day of his alternate universe travel and the 10th day after taking up the investigation, Arjun visited Kavitha's villa as usual. Kavitha, the brilliant scientist with secrets of her own, had become an integral part of his inquiry. The visits were supposed to be discreet, but the ever-watchful media had noticed. Whispers began to arise, questioning the nature of their relationship.

By this third day, Arjun's regular presence at the villa was no longer a secret. He returned, following another lead, and soon after, he found himself spending nights there. The villa, with its advanced security systems and secluded location, became a strategic base for his investigation. Yet, to the outside world, it painted a different picture.

The first murmurs appeared in one of the so-called social media online news feeds, subtle and speculative. "Why is Officer Arjun at Kavitha Pratap's villa again and again?" one post questioned. "Something's fishy," another commented.

Despite the growing buzz, Arjun remained undeterred. The case he was working on was unlike any other—a series of murders that seemed to defy logic and science. Kavitha's knowledge and insights were crucial, and her villa offered a sanctuary where they could work undisturbed by the prying eyes of the world.

On that day, while they were planning to get started with the journey to the other universe, Arjun's phone beeped. It was a message from Manoj. Arjun checked it and it was a forwarded link to that online newspaper and just one line -" need to talk" along with a winking smiley.

Arjun laughed and passed it on to Kavitha, showing her the news about their relationship status. She laughed, returning his mirth, and commented on their newfound celebrity status.

"Well, we might become the talk of the town shortly, right?," she replied dryly, raising one amused eyebrow.

Arjun smiled right back at it. "Can't argue against the fact that we are quite a pair," he said with a friendly smile. "But enough of the gossip; it's time to find out what this dark secret of Mohit and Neeta's world is all about."

With nods that passed between them, they both agreed to leave the rest of the world behind to focus on the mysteries waiting for them on the other side of the thin divide.

Their minds clicked smoothly, readily, into the drill of prepping for the trip, again, across the tremendous cosmic divide, as they were raring to learn the secrets hidden in the shadows of yet another universe. In no time, they were on the other side.

•••

Arjun had been navigating his new alternate life as Mohit, with a sense of purpose and careful calculation. His unusual behavior over the past few days had not gone unnoticed by his family. His mother, father, and brother all had their suspicions, and it was only a matter of time before one of them confronted him.

Arjun was rushing out of the house after his daily breakfast, when his mother, Priya, called him back. "Mohit, could you come to the living room for a moment? I'd like to talk to you," she said, her voice gentle yet firm.

Arjun, maintaining his composure as Mohit, nodded and followed her into the spacious living room was something that surprised her. The room, adorned with family photographs and expensive decor, felt both familiar and alien to him. He sat on the plush sofa, looking at Mohit's mother with a mix of anticipation and concern.

"Mohit, you've been acting differently these past few days," Priya began, her eyes searching his face for any signs of the son she knew. "You're not going out as much, you're more thoughtful, and you're engaging in conversations with us in a way you never did before. What's going on?"

Arjun paused, taking a moment to gather his thoughts. "I've been reflecting a lot lately, Mom. On life, my future, and the person I want to become. It's like I'm seeing things from a new perspective."

Priya raised an eyebrow, both surprised and relieved. "That's a positive change, Mohit. But it seems so sudden. And what about Neeta? Your relationship with her seems to be evolving quickly."

Arjun's expression softened as he thought about how to proceed. He suddenly realized that Mohit might be starting a relationship with

Neeta. "Neeta is... unique. She's different from anyone I've known. There's a connection there that I haven't felt before."

Priya listened carefully. "She does seem like a nice person, Mohit. But I hope you're taking your time. This is new territory for you, and you've always been more relaxed about relationships."

Arjun nodded in agreement. "I understand, Mom. But this is different. With Neeta, I feel like I can be completely open. She's been a positive influence on me. You know....."

He stopped abruptly as he got a call from Shafna and Arjun excused himself from the conversation to take the call "Sorry Mom, I gotta take this"

"Mohit, I need you to come to my apartment immediately, I got a hit on one of the searches" Shafna's voice buzzed over the phone. He said bye to Mom and rushed out which was not at all a surprise to his mother. Once Arjun settled in his car, he quickly pulled out his phone and dialed Kavitha's number.

As soon as she answered, he spoke with urgency, "Kavitha, I just got an urgent call from Shafna. Something seems to be up, and I need to head over there right away. Can you get ready quickly? I'll swing by and pick you up on the way."

He waited for her response.

"Yes come. I'll be ready by then."

He added, "Please be quick; it sounds important."

When Arjun and Kavitha entered Shafna's apartment, she expressed her frustration, "Mohit, I called you last night to inform you immediately, but you were like, 'Who asked for these details?' I was totally confused. Too much drinking nowadays, right?"

Arjun glanced at Kavitha. Kavitha interrupted, trying to smooth things over. "I'm sure he didn't mean anything by it, Shafna. Let's focus on the facts we've got."

Seeing Neeta along with Mohit itself was a surprise to Shafna, but she continued, without asking anything, as she knew how Mohit might react if questioned.

"Alright, anyway look, we got an alert from the system, late last night," Shafna began, pointing at the monitor.

She continued, "Okay, so one of these people has been identified and spotted by the surveillance camera at the parking lot near the Saudi Mosque in Sharjah. With his car plate details, I managed to get his details. His name is Sheikh Omar Mohammad Al Ahmadi and he is an Emirati, a Sheikh." Both looked at the screen carefully and immediately understood that Sheikh Omar was the alternate personality of Prof. Amit Mathur.

"He might be unapproachable, whatever your purpose is" Shafna cautioned.

"Mohit's power and influence can do anything," Kavitha suggested.

"That's a good point. Let's use it to our advantage," Arjun agreed. Shafna found it odd that they were discussing Mohit as if he were a third person. However, sensing her confusion and to avoid any confrontation, Arjun smoothly shifted the conversation to another topic.

Arjun and Kavitha collected the address details from Shafna and left immediately, even though she asked him if he could stay back.

Both Arjun and Kavitha were happy to see that their efforts had started turning out to be fruitful but still not able to figure out how to find the common links.

After meeting Shafna, on the way back to Mohit's office, Kavitha got a WhatsApp message from '**Psycho brother**'. She checked the phone and found it to be a photo message from Neeta's brother. It was an old picture of him with young Neeta. She studied the picture closely, "WHAT THE FUCK!" she shouted as she realized that her brother in this universe was Alex's alternate personality.

"My boyfriend there is my brother here. This is not happening. I can't imagine this, Oh My God" she muttered to herself.

Arjun, seeing this, started laughing initially, but stopped when he saw that she was not taking it as a joke. For some moments, Arjun learned that she was not the jovial Kavitha he had seen till now. She was totally down. Arjun stopped at a coffee shop to give her some time to settle down. While there, he did a search using the photo of the 'Psycho Brother', and found his name and details from his social media profiles. His name was Vineet Joseph, a doctor and he had been in UAE for almost 20 years. They did some more research on him and afterward, they decided to make a visit to meet him.

Arjun disguised himself as a delivery guy and called Vineet from his phone, successfully obtaining the location.

They met him at his villa. He was a doctor, a psychiatrist to be specific, and a bit out-of-the-box person. It seemed like he had great love and care for Neeta. And within some time, they learned that he was half-crazy in his behavior as well as thoughts. After getting close to him, they tried explaining everything to him, but initially, he was skeptical.

"Are you both insane?" he scoffed, shaking his head.

With considerable effort, particularly from Kavitha, who explained her research and the science behind it, they were eventually able to convey the idea to Vineet. Still, he was not ready to accept this new concept completely.

However, after spending some time with her, he began to notice the differences in this "Neeta" sitting before him. She behaved quite differently from his sister Neeta, whom he had known all his life and was very close to. The subtle changes in her demeanor and the way she spoke were undeniable. Being a practitioner of parapsychology & who is interested in studies on extraordinary phenomena, he was naturally curious and sceptical at first. But as he observed these differences more closely, he began to believe the situation. His expertise in studying unusual occurrences made him more open to the possibility, and he agreed to help, eager to understand what was truly happening.

They showed him the drawings of all the victims. Understanding the seriousness of the situation, he carefully studied each picture one after another. While he couldn't recognize most of them, his expression changed when he saw Sofiya Ahmed's photo.

Arjun noticed and pressed him, "Do you know her?"

Vineet hesitated. "No, I don't."

Arjun didn't believe him, but he let it go for the moment. Arjun and Kavitha were planning to leave, but Vineet insisted on having lunch together, which they agreed to, anticipating to get any more details from him about any of the others.

As the conversation progressed, Vineet began asking Kavitha questions, eager to learn more about the technology used for alternate universe travel. Kavitha, very carefully, gave out only limited details as she knew the repercussions of its misuse.

Later, after the late lunch, he went along with Arjun for a smoke outside the villa, and suddenly, while only both of them were there, Vineet confessed.

"The photo you showed of that lady, she is a masseur at an infamous massage center in Bur Dubai. Her name is Jasmin, and I think she's from Thailand. I couldn't say it in front of my sister. It's embarrassing. And I hope you can keep it under wraps."

Arjun took note of the name and details of the massage center and thanked Vineet for his honesty.

As it was already going to be night,- Arjun and Kavitha excused themselves from Vineet and rushed to their own houses to sleep and prepare for the journey back.

Within a couple of minutes, both woke up in their universe at Kavitha's villa. After having a strong coffee, Arjun rushed to his hotel apartment and from there to the station thinking what was waiting for him today on the case here.

Manoj's curiosity about the relationship between Arjun and Kavitha couldn't be contained any longer. At the station, as they settled into the worn-out leather chairs of Arjun's dimly lit office, he decided it was time to address it directly.

"Bro, did you check out the link I sent you about the rumor of you and Kavitha"

"Yes, I did"

"In that case, can I ask you something? "

"Sure Man"

"Is something going on between you and Kavitha? You are never available during evenings for catchups anymore like we used to at the The Black Rock. So, tell me what is it that you are hiding from me?"

Arjun looked up from his cluttered desk, a mix of reports and files that mirrored the chaotic nature of their investigation. He met Manoj's gaze seriously and decided it was time to disclose more about his investigation. "Manoj, there's something I need to tell you, but you have to promise it won't leave this room."

Manoj leaned forward, intrigued. "Of course, Arjun. You know you can trust me."

Arjun took a deep breath. "I'm following an out-of-the-box investigation model. It's complicated, but it's the only way I can see to connect the dots in this case within the given deadline."

Manoj was taken aback, trying to grasp the enormity of what Arjun was saying. "And what is that?"

Arjun leaned in, lowering his voice. "I have been traveling to an alternate universe with the help of Kavitha and her research on quantum mechanics and her experimental technology. It allows me to travel between parallel universes, gathering information from different versions of our world. It's risky, and I wouldn't share this with anyone else, but I need you to believe in it as I do."

Manoj's initial shock gave way to intrigue. He had known Arjun for years, and if anyone else had told him this, he would have dismissed it as madness. But knowing Arjun's meticulous nature and his drive to uncover the truth, Manoj felt a spark of belief. "If anyone else had told me this, I'd think they were crazy. But knowing you, Arjun, I'll take your word for it. How does it work exactly?"

Arjun relaxed slightly, seeing Manoj's willingness to understand. "It's complex. There's a compound that allows for this kind of travel, but it requires precise calibration and an immense amount of energy. Kavitha and I have been working on this for days now. It's how we've been able to gather such unique insights into our case."

Manoj nodded slowly, trying to wrap his head around the concept. "So, you're saying there are parallel versions of us, of this world?"

"Exactly," Arjun confirmed. "And by traveling to these alternate realities, we can see different outcomes, different paths taken. It's like having multiple vantage points on the same problem. And we believe that we will be able to find the murderer there by finding this vantage points."

Manoj's mind raced with the possibilities. "So, what have you found out so far?"

Arjun leaned back, the weight of the information he carried evident in his eyes. "A lot, actually. The murderer's and victims' personalities and connections with each other in the other universe — everything starts making more sense when you see the bigger picture. Kavitha's been a crucial part of this, helping to keep everything in balance."

Manoj was silent for a moment, absorbing the gravity of what Arjun had shared. "This explains a lot about your recent behavior. The late nights, the secrecy... Man, it's mind boggling!"

Arjun met his gaze with unwavering trust. "Anyway, thanks for initiating this discussion. I was wondering how I will disclose this to you because I need your help, Manoj. Going forward, we need to complement the investigations in both universes with each other. I can't do this alone. And more importantly, I trust you. You're one of the few people I know who can handle this information without jumping to conclusions or letting it cloud their judgment."

Manoj felt a surge of responsibility. "Alright, Arjun. I'm in. Let's sit down and analyze our findings from both universes."

They spent the next few hours piecing together clues, cross-referencing their discoveries from this universe and the alternate one. The room was filled with the soft rustling of papers and the hum of the computer as they sifted through data, the occasional murmur of conversation breaking the silence.

Arjun pulled up a series of images, created by Kavitha, on his screen, pointing out the similarities and differences between the universes. Manoj was surprised to see the similarities between the alternate personalities of the victims. Ignoring that, Arjun continued, "Look at this. In both realities, the victims have a common link—a hidden connection that we wouldn't have seen if we were looking at just one version of events."

Manoj leaned in, studying the images closely. "You're right. And this detail here—it's only present in the alternate universe. It's like a piece of a puzzle we didn't even know we were missing."

Arjun nodded. "Exactly. And there's more. The killer's methods, the way they choose their victims—it's all tied to something deeper, something we haven't fully understood yet. But with this new perspective, we're getting closer."

Manoj sat back, processing the information. "One thing's for sure," he said, rubbing his temples. "The killer is definitely a guy. All our findings in 'this universe' point to that. May be if it is of any use for your search in the other universe"

Arjun agreed, his expression grim. "Yes, ofcourse that's a major point and this can help in getting closer. With this new perspective, I may be able to narrow the search for common connections there and we might just crack the case wide open."

They continued their discussion late into the afternoon, the complexity of their investigation only matched by their determination to uncover the truth. The hours flew by as they theorized, debated, and re-examined every piece of evidence. Each discovery led to more questions, but also to more clarity.

At one point, Manoj paused, staring at a photograph of one of the victims. “Arjun, do you ever wonder what drives someone to do this? To cross such a line?”

Arjun sighed, his eyes reflecting the weight of their task. “Every day, Manoj. But I think in this case, it’s more than just a twisted mind. There’s something deeper at play—something almost...dangerously strange.”

They fell into a thoughtful silence, the enormity of their task hanging heavy in the air. The room seemed to close in around them, the walls lined with evidence that told a story far more complex than they had ever imagined.

Eventually, Manoj broke the silence. “So, what’s our next move?”

Arjun looked at him, determination hardening his features. “We keep digging. We analyze every piece of data from both universes, looking for any inconsistencies or patterns. As soon as I find the common connections there, I need you to find the alternates of them here. Keep all your resources ready for that search. Meanwhile, we need to do our investigation to keep going here also.”

Manoj nodded, feeling a renewed sense of purpose. “Alright. Let’s get to work.”

Manoj made a couple of calls to different teams and made sure everything was set and ready to be activated. Arjun took the case updates from his team and gave them the instructions for the further steps and actions from their side.

By evening, both of them were totally clear on the steps ahead. Arjun to continue his pursuit along with Kavitha through their perilous journeys between universes, gathering more data and insights. And

Manoj's part was to stay behind, coordinating efforts to work here utilizing the information they brought back, along with continuing on his own path of investigations.

CHAPTER 13

WHISPERS IN THE SHADOWS

As the evening deepened and the streetlights flickered to life, Arjun's car cut through the quiet streets, heading towards Kavitha's villa for what felt like an endless series of trips. His thoughts were heavy, the weight of recent events pressing down on him.

Just then his phone buzzed, the screen lighting up with a video call from Divya. It came to his mind that he hadn't called Divya in days. Though he hadn't felt her absence while entangled with Shafna and the web of mysteries he was trying to unravel, a nagging guilt gnawed at him now.

With a deep breath, he accepted the call, her familiar smile instantly appearing on the screen.

"Good evening, Arjun! How's everything going?" Divya's voice was warm, her energy lifting his spirits momentarily.

"Evening, Divya. Just another busy day. How about you?" Arjun replied, trying to mask the guilt lingering in his chest.

"Work, meetings, the usual chaos," she said with a light laugh. "Oh, did you get a chance to look at the gift I sent you?"

"Yeah, I did. It's beautiful. Thanks, love," Arjun said, though his mind was only half present.

"Don't forget to make some time for me too," she teased, but Arjun could sense the seriousness beneath her words.

"I will. I promise," he nodded, though his thoughts were already drifting back to the case.

Their conversation flowed with ease, but something she said suddenly sparked an idea that pierced through the fog clouding Arjun's mind. Divya mentioned a detective show she'd been watching, how the detectives would find hidden connections between people—relationships no one else noticed, trails of evidence overlooked by the untrained eye.

Arjun's heart raced. Could that be the key? The missing piece that could tie everything together? Maybe a detective agency could uncover the connections he hadn't yet seen, could dig into the tangled mess of people, places, and events that were beginning to overwhelm him.

"That's actually... really interesting," Arjun muttered, his tone shifting. "You just gave me an idea."

"What kind of idea?" Divya asked, curious.

"I'll explain later," he said hurriedly. "I need to go, but thanks for the chat, Divya. You've really helped."

"Alright, talk to you later, baby. Have a good night!"

"You too, Divya. Take care," Arjun responded, ending the call with a smile.

As he ended the call, Arjun's mind raced with the new plan. The idea of hiring a detective agency, something he hadn't considered before, now seemed like the breakthrough he needed. He couldn't shake the feeling that this was the right move—the path that would finally lead him to the truth.

Arjun's car slowly stopped in front of Kavitha's villa, a familiar sight now, nestled quietly in the shadows of the night. He parked and stepped out, his mind still racing from the sudden idea that Divya had unintentionally sparked during their call. Could hiring a detective agency really be the key? The missing piece to unraveling the tangled connections between the various characters, and the mystery that haunted?

He stood still for a moment, breathing in the cool night air. The idea simmered in his thoughts as he approached the front door of the villa. The place had become his second home, a refuge where he and Kavitha could strategize and plan their journeys to the alternate universe.

The villa's large doors swung open as Kavitha greeted him, her eyes tired but determined. "You're late," she said, but there was no annoyance in her tone. She understood the weight Arjun carried, and the exhaustion on his face mirrored her own.

"Yeah, had a call with Divya on the way here. She mentioned something that might help us. I'll tell you about it later," Arjun said, stepping inside. The villa, with its modern interior and technological setup, felt like the only place where their unusual reality made sense.

Kavitha led him to the living room where the equipment for their alternate universe travel was already set up. Over the past few days, this had become their routine—reviewing the day's findings, planning their next steps, and then slipping into the alternate world to continue their investigation. The travel process, once foreign and daunting, had now become as routine as any other task. But tonight, something felt different.

"Everything's ready for the journey today," Kavitha said, settling into her chair. "Today, we don't have time to do any discussions, and let's do it once we reach there. Let's go."

Arjun glanced at the clock. It was nearing midnight. Time in both worlds seemed to blur together lately, with no clear boundary between day and night. His life had become an endless cycle of investigation, alternate realities, and shifting perspectives. Arjun sat down, rubbing his temple. The back-and-forth between realities had been exhausting, but it was their only hope of solving this case.

"Ready?" Kavitha asked. As usual, she carefully got the injection ready and calibrated the equipment, her fingers hovering over the controls.

Arjun nodded. "Let's go."

The familiar sensation washed over him as his consciousness drifted away from the villa. Moments later, he opened his eyes, finding himself once again in the alternate universe, where he was Mohit.

In this world, he had learned to navigate Mohit's life—his relationships, his routines, and the dark secrets that lay just beneath the surface. Each trip provided them with more clues, more pieces of the puzzle they were trying to solve.

As Mohit, Arjun moved with purpose through his luxurious home, heading to the office where he knew Neeta would be waiting. She had emerged as a central figure in this world, her support being of utmost importance in finding the deep connections..

Neeta looked up as he entered the room, her eyes filled with both suspicion and curiosity. "You're late," she said, echoing Kavitha's earlier words.

"I know," Arjun replied, settling into Mohit's chair. "We've got a lot to discuss. But before we start, let's go over what we've got so far."

They laid out the notes they had gathered from both universes: connections between the victims, the personalities they took on in the alternate universe, and the strange coincidences that were beginning to form a web too complex to ignore.

They meticulously examined the findings from the previous day, carefully reviewing every detail. Arjun had grown adept at balancing both universes, keeping his mind sharp even as the complexities of the case threatened to overwhelm him.

"So, here's the thing," Arjun began, leaning forward. "In this universe, while we are winning on one side by being able to find the alternate personalities of the victims, we're hitting walls with this investigation on the other side as we are still not able to make out how to find their common connections. I've been thinking that maybe we need outside help."

Kavitha raised an eyebrow. "Outside help? From who?"

"A detective agency," Arjun said, the idea sounding more solid as he voiced it. "This is the idea which I mentioned I received during my call with Divya." He continued, "Think about it. They specialize in digging up connections and finding hidden links that aren't obvious to us. We're too close to this; we need a fresh perspective, someone who can work behind the scenes while we handle things here and in our universe."

Kavitha's gaze sharpened. "You think a detective agency could find something we've missed?"

"It's worth a shot. We've been focusing on the surface—the murders, the personal motives in our universe and finding the alternate personalities of them in here. But there's a bigger connection here, and I think they could help us see it."

Kavitha nodded, her mind already working through the logistics. "I see your point. They actually could dig up the connections in this universe and that can be a deal breaker for us."

"Exactly," Arjun said. "We have to cover all our bases. This investigation spans two realities. We can't afford to miss anything."

Kavitha leaned back, a faint smile crossing her lips. "You always come up with the craziest ideas, but this one... it might actually work." After a pause, she continued, "But, how will we give out the details for them to start with? We can't exactly tell them about our alternate lives."

Arjun smiled slightly. "We don't have to. As far as I know, professional detective agencies never ask for the motives, they just have to be briefed on what we want... and the payment. So, we can provide them with the leads we've gathered and let them take it from there and we can always give a story as a reason, in case."

Kavitha nodded, seeing the logic in the plan. "That could work. We'll need to be careful about how much we reveal. We don't want to jeopardize our investigation or our cover."

With the plan set in motion, they turned their attention back to the new task at hand: finding the best detective agency there.

"We need to act fast," Arjun said, his voice filled with urgency. "We don't have much time."

Kavitha nodded; her expression grim. "We'll do whatever it takes. I will work on finding the detective agency and you can work on the details to be handed over to them"

As Kavitha left Mohit's office and returned to the now familiar workspace of Neeta, she realized that their next move would be crucial. The detective agency would help unravel the connections in their world, but now, it is up to her to find the key to the next step. She started doing her research on the top-performing detective agencies.

Arjun's heart pounded in his chest as he stood, the weight of the case pressing down on him. He had never felt so close to the truth, yet so far from it at the same time.

The detective agency would be crucial in finding the connections in their own universe, while he and Kavitha continued their investigation. Every step they took brought them closer to uncovering the conspiracy, but the danger was growing with each passing moment. With these thoughts, he started his part of the job.

By noontime, Kavitha entered Mohit's cabin with a victorious smile on her lips. Whereas, Arjun also seemed to have reached the goal, but was tired from relentless brainstorming on how and what to convey to the agency to get it done.

Arjun leaned back in his chair, looking at her. "Seems you hit the bull's eye"

"Yes," she replied, pulling out the printout of a brochure. "Blackstone Investigations. They have a reputation for handling high-profile and complex cases. Their team includes experts in forensics, cybercrime, and undercover operations. The only thing is that they seem to be quite expensive."

"Leave the cost part, as Mohit's money can take care of it", mentioned Arjun while taking the printout of the brochure from her, skimming through the details. *Blackstone Investigations, based in the dynamic city of Dubai, is a covert detective agency formed by an elite team of retired FBI agents and retired investigators from around the world. Specializing in high-stakes cases with global implications, the agency's operations remain as discreet as they are effective. Leading the charge is Andrew Philips, an ex-FBI agent with an impeccable track record in solving complex, high-profile cases. Known for his observation, sharp intuition, and relentless pursuit of the truth, Philips brings a wealth of experience and a network of local as well as international contacts, making Blackstone Investigations a formidable force in global crime-solving.*

"They seem like the right fit."

"Agreed," she said, sitting down across from him. "I have already made the call and have set up the meeting with their lead detective, Andrew. He will be here at sharp 4 PM. We can meet him here in your office. It's neutral ground, and we can control the narrative."

"Perfect," Arjun replied. "We'll be ready."

Kavitha nodded in agreement, feeling a renewed sense of hope. "Let's do it. The sooner we get them involved, the better our chances of solving this case fast."

Arjun couldn't help but feel a sense of relief. They were finally getting the help they needed.

Just then, the intercom buzzed, breaking his concentration.

"Mr. Mohit, Mr. Mukul from Al Farrah Technologies is here for the meeting," the receptionist's voice came through.

Arjun's heart raced. He wasn't prepared for this. Trying to avoid it, he asked "He doesn't have an appointment, does he?". Just opposite to the answer he was expecting, Shagufta replied instantaneously "Yes of course. You wanted to have this meeting and this was scheduled for today at 3:30 PM, almost 2 weeks back Mr. Mohit.", in a confused tone.

Taking a deep breath, he pressed the button to respond. "Please tell Mukul that I'm caught up in an urgent matter and will need to reschedule. Make sure he understands it's unavoidable."

"Understood, sir," she replied. Arjun could hear the hesitance in her voice but knew he had no choice. He had to avoid this meeting at all costs, to avoid any suspicion. For a couple of days while in Mohit's disguise, the only thing Arjun was doing was signing documents and cheques while at the office.

Anyway, having sorted that, they went back to what they were working on.

As 4 PM approached, Arjun and Kavitha prepared the office, organizing the files and setting up the notes they had collected. When Andrew arrived, the receptionist greeted him warmly, leading him into Mohit's office.

As Andrew stepped into the room, his tall, lean frame exuded quiet confidence. His neutral expression revealed little, save for a slight, almost imperceptible smile that softened the edges of his otherwise stern demeanor. His sharp, observant eyes scanned the room with calculated precision, taking in every detail, from the subtle shift in the lighting to the unspoken tension between the two people seated before him. It was a trait honed over years of investigations, one that never failed to serve him well.

Arjun, now in his alternate identity as Mohit, and Kavitha, disguised as Neeta, shifted in their seats. The receptionist had announced them under their assumed names, but as they spoke to each other, old habits slipped through.

Kavitha greeted Andrew and said, "Arjun, this is Andrew from Blackstone Investigations."

"Good afternoon, Andrew," Arjun began, directing him to the seat very politely, "Thank you for meeting with us on such short notice. Hope Kavitha didn't push you too much for meeting today itself."

Andrew nodded, taking a seat. "Good afternoon. And hey, No problem. Such short notice meetings are usual for me, as most of the clients would be in a hurry."

Meanwhile, Andrew's eyes flicked up at the mention of the names, his mind piecing it together without missing a beat. His expression remained unchanged as he casually leaned against the desk, hands in his pockets. His smile faded just slightly as he made his first observation aloud.

"Strange," Andrew said, his voice calm yet deliberate. "The receptionist mentioned you as Mohit and Neeta, but you two seem quite comfortable using different names."

The comment hung in the air for a moment, but Andrew quickly waved it off with a dismissive shrug, his tone lightening. "But hey, that's none of my business. People have all kinds of reasons for keeping secrets." His eyes locked onto them, sharp and unwavering, his neutral smile returning. "Now, tell me what you need me to do. I'm guessing it's something you wouldn't want just anyone to handle."

Without skipping a beat, Andrew's focus shifted fully onto the task at hand, ready to delve into the mystery they were about to lay before him.

Both Arjun and Kavitha, were shocked at the mention of names by Andrew, understanding their own mistake, but felt relieved by the view of Andrew. But, going forward, both made sure to stick on to calling each other the correct names, Mohit and Neeta.

Arjun took the lead, handing over the photos, along with the names and addresses of the people, they have found till date through Shafna - Ala Mohammad, Jasmin, Manish Singh, Sheikh Omar Mohammad

Al Ahmadi, and Vineet Joseph. Further, Arjun clearly explained what they are looking for from Andrew's team to investigate - any person and/or persons with whom all these 4 have common connections. While Arjun started to narrate his 'cooked-up story' as the reason for this requirement, Andrew stopped him abruptly saying," We don't ask 'Why', we just need to know what's required and that you have already briefed me."

Andrew continued after a small pause, "You will get the invoice by mail within max 10 minutes. Just pay the 50% as advance. As soon as we receive the funds, my team and I will go through everything you've gathered and begin our investigation. You'll be kept in the loop with regular updates.". He said bye and left the office.

Arjun and Kavitha were sure of one thing. This guy is going to be a key factor in their investigation.

After Andrew left, Arjun sat at his desk, trying to crack the case in his mind, looking for any possible connections but to no avail. Even though the detective agency was put on the job, there was no time to waste and he wanted to utilize every second to rush towards the discovery.

Just then, he got the mail from Blackstone Investigations with the invoice for quite an enormous amount. Smilingly, he took out Mohit's personal account cheque book which was kept pre-signed and wrote a cheque for the advance amount, and handed it over to Kavitha to send it through the messenger immediately.

As the day wore on, Arjun's thoughts drifted back to Divya, to the moment on the call when everything had clicked. Her casual mention of a detective show had sparked an idea that could change the course of their investigation. He would have to thank her later, once this was all over.

For now, though, there was only the case. The lives at stake. And the thin line between two worlds that held the answers they so desperately needed.

While he was getting ready to leave the office, he received a call from Shafna," Hey Mohit, you want to try the best Karak tea in Dubai? Not from your usual posh hangout places, this is a small tea shop in Mamzar. Maybe we can chit chat also. I'll be there at 08:30. See you there."

Without giving a chance for Arjun to reply, she completed and disconnected the phone. He hesitated for a moment noting the fact that he would be late for the travel back, but at the same time, he didn't want to make Shafna unhappy as she was an important part in solving this riddle.

Involuntarily, he called Kavitha and informed about this meeting and asked her also to join," It's already 07:30 PM, let's push off noting the traffic towards that area." he continued after a pause, "Or you go down and just wait near the car. I have something to do at the reception and then I will join you."

Arjun made his way to the reception area expecting to get hold of the receptionist. Shagufta, the ever-observant receptionist, greeted him with a curious look.

"Good evening, Mr. Mohit, oops sorry, just Mohit, Busy day?" she asked, a hint of amusement in her voice.

Arjun nodded, attempting to mimic Mohit's usual demeanor. "Yes, very. By the way, have you heard anything interesting around here lately?"

Shagufta's eyes sparkled with the opportunity to share the latest gossip. "Oh, you know how it is. Office talk never stops. But there's one thing that's caught everyone's attention."

Arjun leaned in slightly, encouraging her to continue. "Really? What's that?"

"Well," Shagufta began, lowering her voice, "there are some rumors about you and Neeta. People have noticed you two spending a lot of time together outside the office. They're saying you're always seen together these days."

Arjun felt a mix of confusion and curiosity. This was something he hadn't anticipated. "Interesting. And what exactly are they saying?"

Shagufta shrugged, clearly enjoying her role as the bearer of juicy tidbits. "Just the usual speculations. Some think there's more to your relationship than just work. Others are just curious about why you're always seen together. You know how people are."

Arjun nodded thoughtfully, his mind racing. He needed to tread carefully. "Well, you know how rumors are, Shagufta. Often baseless and blown out of proportion. Thanks for the heads-up."

She smiled, clearly pleased to be in the loop. "Of course, Mohit. Just thought you'd want to know."

As Arjun walked away, he couldn't shake the feeling that this new piece of information might be crucial. He needed to learn more about Mohit's interactions with Neeta and ensure his cover remained intact. The office was a minefield of secrets and rumors, and navigating it required more than just a good disguise.

•••

Arjun and Kavitha arrived at the karak tea shop by around 8:40. Shafna was already there, sitting at a corner table in the open-air section, her fingers tapping lightly on the table's edge. When she spotted Kavitha walking beside Arjun, a flicker of surprise crossed her face—she hadn't expected Kavitha to be here, and certainly not with him. Still, she masked her reaction with a quick smile and waved them over.

"I told you, this place has the best karak tea in all of Dubai," Shafna said as they settled into their chairs, breaking the initial awkward silence. "It's the kind of place where you'll see everyone—from CEOs to construction workers—just for the tea." She gestured around at the mix of people, clearly proud of the shop's reputation.

She caught the eye of a young man near the counter, Munna, and called him over with a familiar nod. "Three specials, please." It was obvious she was a regular; Munna gave a friendly nod and hurried off to prepare the order.

The conversation started slowly, each of them dancing around topics that didn't touch any nerves. There was a palpable awkwardness in the air—like none of them were quite sure why they were sitting together—but soon enough, the stiffness thawed. A few laughs were exchanged over shared stories, and by the time the tea arrived, they were discussing books, travel, and restaurants with an easy familiarity.

As Shafna took a sip of her steaming tea, she suddenly leaned forward, lowering her voice. "So, those names and details I managed to get you... did they help?" she asked.

Kavitha froze mid-sip, and Arjun's eyes widened. Shafna caught their reaction and tilted her head, frowning slightly. "What's going on, Mohit?" she said, her voice edged with suspicion. "You're not... caught up in something weird, are you?"

"No, no," Arjun said quickly, forcing a chuckle. "It's nothing like that. We just needed the information for... a project, something business-related." He hoped the vague explanation would be enough.

Shafna's expression softened, but her eyes still held a hint of doubt. "Sure, sure," she said, leaning back with a half-smile. "You two have been thick as thieves lately, so I thought I'd tease you a bit. Partners in crime, huh?" Her tone was playful, but a note of jealousy crept into her voice.

They all laughed, but Kavitha could sense the tension lingering just beneath the surface. Shafna didn't look entirely convinced.

As if sensing the shift, Munna returned to their table, checking to see if they needed anything. Before they could respond, a voice called out from the far end of the shop. Munna turned, and they all followed his gaze. A woman in her thirties, wearing a blue kurti and jeans, stood near the entrance.

"Hi, Vidya Ma'am!" Munna called back, rushing to meet her.

Arjun and Kavitha exchanged a startled glance. In unison, they muttered, "Aparna Devi?" It was like the name had sprung to both their minds at the exact same moment.

"What's that?" Shafna asked, puzzled.

Arjun hesitated, then pointed towards the woman. "The lady in the blue... she looks familiar. Do you know who she is?"

Shafna shook her head, curiosity sparking in her eyes. "No, but I can find out." She pulled out her phone, snapping a discreet picture of the woman, and began typing furiously into an app. After a few seconds, she grinned triumphantly and held up the screen. "Got it. Her name is Vidya Jairaj. Want the full details?"

Arjun leaned in, reading off the profile that popped up. "Vidya Jairaj, originally from Kerala, was born and raised in Dubai. Works as a planning engineer at a construction firm. Single, and it had her address and other details." He quickly forwarded the information to himself.

"Impressed?" Shafna asked, laughing. "You two clearly underestimate me. Now, as a reward, you're buying me another tea." She flashed a teasing smile.

Arjun chuckled, playing along, but his mind was racing. He and Kavitha exchanged another brief glance before she turned her attention back to Vidya, who was talking animatedly with Munna by the counter. Kavitha observed the easy rapport between them—the way Vidya rested a hand on Munna's shoulder, laughing at something he said. They seemed like old friends, or maybe something closer like siblings. It was a rare, genuine warmth that caught Kavitha's attention.

After a while, Kavitha glanced at her watch and nudged Arjun. It was getting late. They made their excuses, saying goodbye to Shafna, who still looked like she had more questions bubbling just below the surface.

On the way back, as soon as they started, Kavitha was already typing out a quick message to Andrew, forwarding the details they'd gathered. By the time both reached back at their respective homes, it was already around 1 AM. They immediately went to sleep, expecting to wake up in the other universe.

•••

Arjun jolted awake in Kavitha's villa, blinking up at the ceiling. He lay still for a moment, disoriented by the familiar strangeness of returning to his own universe. The sun was already high, light streaming through the wide windows. He fumbled for his phone and checked the time—8:00 AM. Too late, but he felt as though he hadn't slept at all. The transitions always left him exhausted, a heavy fatigue settling in his bones that he couldn't quite shake.

From across the room, Kavitha looked up from her desk, where she was poring over a stack of documents, pen in hand. She observed him with a mix of concern and curiosity. "Rough morning?" she asked, raising an eyebrow. Her face, though alert, showed the faint shadows of exhaustion as well.

Arjun gave a weary nod. "Tired isn't the word," he muttered, rubbing his temples.

Kavitha nodded knowingly. "It's because we stayed up late in the other universe," she said, leaning back in her chair. "You know, sometimes you wake up tired here even after a full night's sound sleep? It's because some version of you, in any of the alternate universes, might have had a wild night out or pulled an all-nighter. It all... bleeds through." She gave a small, humorless laugh. "Guess it caught up to us this time."

He took in her words, not entirely convinced but too tired to argue. "Well, if that's true, my 'other self' needs to stop partying."

Kavitha chuckled, but her amusement was short-lived. She handed him a strong cup of coffee, which he took gratefully, hoping it would shake off the lingering fatigue. After finishing his coffee and exchanging a few more words with her, he left the villa, heading back to his hotel to freshen up.

An hour later, Arjun arrived at the station. The familiar buzz of activity and the hum of voices greeted him as he spotted the team gathered near the briefing room. Manoj was in the middle of detailing something to Maya and Rajiv when he looked up and waved Arjun over.

"Perfect timing," Manoj said, handing him a file. "This is everything Rajiv got from Allookkara."

Arjun nodded, flipping open the file and taking in the first few lines. Whatever fatigue he felt faded into the background as he focused, ready to dive back into the investigation.

Going through the report by Rajiv, Arjun felt a mix of anticipation and frustration. The day had become long, filled with an overwhelming amount of information to sift through, and Rajiv's report was supposed to bring some clarity. Instead, it brought more questions than answers.

Arjun skimmed through the document, his eyes narrowing as he absorbed the details. Rajiv had done an exhaustive search, interviewing villagers, examining local records, and even visiting the sites where the girl was last seen. Yet, there was no solid lead—no one connected to the missing girl, no familial ties, no friends who could provide insights into her disappearance. She seemed like a ghost, a figment of a story that had already faded into the shadows of the dense jungle.

Arjun sighed, running a hand through his hair. The frustration gnawed at him. Every dead end felt like a personal failure, a step back in their relentless pursuit of the truth. However, amidst the bleak findings, one detail caught his eye.

Rajiv mentioned a local guide, an enigmatic figure who knew about the ancient rituals performed in the jungle. This guide, described as both fearless and knowledgeable, was willing to take them deep into the heart of the jungle. It was a sliver of hope, which might help them to procure a potential breakthrough in a case that seemed to be slipping through their fingers.

"We should head back to Allookkara," Maya suggested, her tone firm. "I still think there are things we missed, especially around the ritual site. We might get more if we press the locals again."

Manoj immediately shook his head, leaning back in his chair. "No," he said, holding up a hand to cut her off. "Rajiv already canvassed the area, Maya. If we go back now, we need something concrete—another visit with vague questions will just tip people off that we're circling them."

Maya's jaw tightened, and she opened her mouth as if to argue, but then shut it, exhaling sharply instead. "Fine," she muttered, crossing her arms.

Rajiv interjected, aiming to lighten the tension. "Maybe we're just missing that one little thread. A fresh lead, even a small one, could make all the difference." He looked at Arjun for input.

But Arjun, still distracted by the report, leaned back in his chair, the weight of the day pressing down on him. He closed his eyes for a moment, trying to gather his thoughts. The idea of venturing into the jungle was both daunting and exhilarating. The rituals mentioned had an eerie, almost mystical quality to them, and Arjun couldn't help but feel a shiver of anticipation at the thought of uncovering their secrets.

He turned to Manoj, his voice low and serious. "Manoj, I need to catch you up on something," he said. He gestured for Rajiv and Maya to step outside, giving them a nod of thanks as they left the room. As they left the room, Arjun shut the door behind them and dropped into the chair opposite Manoj, who folded his arms and leaned forward expectantly.

"Alright," Arjun began, lowering his voice. "There have been some developments in the other universe." Manoj's expression didn't change, but his eyes narrowed, focusing intently.

Arjun continued, "In the alternate universe, we've identified one more person—Vidya Jairaj. She's the alternate personality of Aparna Devi. So, now we have found the alternate personalities of all the six victims. Now I am trying to identify the connections common to all these six, with some help"

"How exactly?" Manoj asked, clearly curious. "You mentioned help."

"A private detective agency," Arjun said, leaning in. "In the other universe, I've involved them to identify the connections. It's... unconventional, I know. But the overlaps between what's happening there and here are getting harder to ignore. If something comes up on that side, it could be the lead we need to move forward here."

Their conversation was interrupted by a knock on the door. It swung open, and Rajiv and Maya stepped back inside, followed closely by Sarah from forensics, holding a tablet in one hand. Maya's face was flushed with excitement.

"We've got a breakthrough," Maya said, barely able to contain her enthusiasm.

Sarah stepped forward, glancing at Arjun. "Remember that envelope you found in Alex Mathew's apartment?" she asked. "We discovered a hair strand stuck inside, seemingly when it was sealed. And we did a DNA profiling of it."

Arjun and Manoj almost jumped out of their chairs., the air suddenly electric with anticipation. "This is a great breakthrough. Great job Arjun" Manoj said, unable to hide the thrill in his voice. Then he turned to Sarah. "Can you brief us on the analysis report, please"

Sarah tapped her tablet and started her explanation, her tone steady but eager. "The DNA profiling indicates the suspect is a male, between 18 and 22 years old. We've digitized the profile, which means we can cross-reference it with any samples we get. If we can match hair, skin, or any biological trace from a suspect, we'll have confirmation."

"This indeed is going to be quite helpful in solving the puzzle", Manoj said, his eyes alight with determination. "Sarah, start running that profile against the DNA samples in our criminal database. Let's see if any matches come up. Rajiv, and Maya, I want you two to assist her—dig through everything we have. I want results as soon as possible."

Sarah nodded, clearly eager to get started, and left with Rajiv and Maya in tow, their voices already blending into a buzz of focused planning as they headed down the hall to the lab.

The door shut behind them, and Arjun turned back to Manoj, the excitement still simmering in his veins. "This changes everything," he said. "If we get a match, we might finally have a face—a direction."

Arjun and Manoj, excited with this finding, continued with strategizing the next steps based on this new revelation.

By noon, the exhaustion had taken its toll. Arjun's head throbbed with a relentless headache, each pulse a reminder of the pressures bearing down on him. He knew he needed to rest, to clear his mind for the challenges that lay ahead. He asked Manoj to carry on and left the station for his apartment. Taking a painkiller, he settled into his chair, hoping for a brief respite from the demands of the investigation.

As he closed his eyes, the sounds of the day faded into a quiet hum. The dim light of the setting sun cast long shadows across his office, creating an atmosphere of eerie calm. Arjun allowed himself to drift into a light sleep, hoping that a power nap would rejuvenate him enough to tackle the next phase of their quest.

CHAPTER 14

BLURRED AND TWISTED

Arjun felt a strange sensation, a dizzying shift as the world around him blurred and twisted. When the disorienting whirl stopped, he blinked and found himself standing in Mohit's cabin. The familiar sight of the office was transformed into something nightmarish. The scene from the big French windows showed a blood-red sky, casting an eerie, crimson glow over everything. The air was thick with tension, and a sense of impending doom hung heavy over everything.

He took a cautious step forward, his heart pounding in his chest. The floor beneath his feet cracked and shifted as if the very ground was unstable. A cold sweat broke out on his forehead as he realized he was not alone. Shadowy figures began to emerge from the gloom, their eyes glowing with a malevolent red light. They moved with a predatory grace, their intentions clear and hostile.

Arjun's breath caught in his throat as they advanced toward him, their forms becoming more defined with each step. He could see their twisted features, grotesque and menacing, as they closed in. His instinct screamed at him to run, but when he turned, the landscape around him morphed violently. Walls of jagged rock sprang up from the ground, blocking his path and trapping him in a small, confined space.

Panic surged through him, his pulse quickening as he found himself cornered. The shadowy figures closed in, their faces contorted in sinister grins. Arjun raised his hands in a futile attempt to defend himself, his mind racing to look for a way out. But there was no escape. They were upon him, their cold hands grasping and pulling him into the darkness.

A piercing scream echoed in his ears, filling his mind with terror. The last thing he saw was their glowing eyes and twisted smiles as they dragged him into the void. Then, everything went black.

Arjun jolted awake, drenched in sweat, his heart racing. He sat up, gasping for breath, trying to shake off the lingering terror of the nightmare. He was in his room, the familiar surroundings a stark contrast to the horrifying dream that felt like the alternate universe he had just escaped from.

He looked at the clock and was shocked to see the time as 08:10 AM. He realized that he had a very long sleep, but couldn't make out what happened to him. He reached out for his phone and saw around 22 missed calls from Kavitha from the previous day till midnight. He called Kavitha asking if she could come immediately. Understanding the seriousness from his voice, Kavitha started immediately and within around 20 minutes, she reached his hotel room. Kavitha rushed to his side. "Arjun, I was wondering why you didn't turn up for the travel yesterday. I was continuously trying to reach you. Are you okay?" she asked, her voice filled with concern.

Arjun nodded, still trying to catch his breath. "It felt so real," he said, his voice shaky. "Seems like I.... I was in the parallel universe, Mohit's world, and some shadowy figures were attacking me. Is it like my conscience traveled to the other universe without any injections? Or is it just a dream? I thought I lost myself for a moment."

Kavitha placed a reassuring hand on his shoulder. "It sounds like your brain is reacting to being overworked. You've been pushing yourself for almost 96 hours without proper rest. Four days of alternate universe travel! This is new for me too—I've never traveled consecutively for this many days. It seems like we need to take a break and get some proper sleep."

Arjun looked around the room, the familiar surroundings slowly bringing him back to reality. The soft glow of the lamp cast comforting shadows, and Kavitha's presence was a grounding force. He nodded, the adrenaline beginning to fade. "You're right. We've already assigned the work to the detective agency. They need a couple of days to carry out their job. We should take a break."

Kavitha smiled in relief. "Exactly. We need to give our brains a rest. And remember the restriction, a maximum of 10 consecutive days of travel at one stretch. After that, we have to wait nearly 10 days before starting another trip."

Arjun leaned back on the couch, letting out a deep sigh. The weight of the past few days seemed to lift slightly, and he felt a wave of exhaustion wash over him. "I guess I didn't realize how much it was affecting me," he admitted.

Kavitha nodded sympathetically. "It's easy to lose track when you're so focused. But we need to take care of ourselves if we're going to solve this case."

She stood up and walked to the kitchen, returning with a glass of water. "Here, drink this. It'll help calm you down."

Arjun took the glass, sipping the cool water gratefully. "Thanks, Kavitha. I don't know what I'd do without you."

"We're a team," she replied, sitting back down next to him. "We look out for each other."

Kavitha saw Arjun's phone ringing. She asked him to stay on the bed and went to get the phone. It was Manoj. She handed over the phone to Arjun.

"Hey, Manoj, what's up?" Arjun asked, still feeling the lingering effects of his nightmare.

"Good morning, buddy, hope you are feeling better now. See, we got a message from the IT team. All the photos, except two, have been developed and AI aged. We're all gathering at the lab to do the matching with the victims' photos. You need to be here," Manoj said, his voice urgent.

Arjun glanced at Kavitha, who nodded in agreement. "I'll be there soon," he told Manoj, ending the call.

Kavitha came near Arjun, "I know that you have to rush. But what about a coffee together, today evening?"

"Kavitha, I would have loved to, but I think we are running out of time and I need to focus completely on the investigations. Maybe we'll do it later."

He quickly gathered the things and hurried to the lab. The corridors seemed longer and more foreboding than usual, but Arjun brushed off the lingering unease from his dream. He entered the lab to find the team already assembled, with a palpable tension in the air.

The room was packed with screens and tables strewn with photos and documents. Following Manoj's instructions, the IT team set up a large display showcasing the newly developed photos alongside the victims' images. Arjun joined the group, his attention immediately captured by the display.

"Alright, let's see what we have," Arjun said, his voice steady but his mind racing with anticipation.

The team began the meticulous process of comparing the photos. Four of the images matched perfectly with the victims' pictures, their identities confirmed with a chilling certainty. Each match was like a piece of a puzzle falling into place, bringing them closer to understanding the horrifying events they were investigating.

"Look at this one," Manoj pointed to one of the two undeveloped photos. It was partially visible, the features blurred but somewhat recognizable. "We think this might be Alex. It's not fully developed, but there's a resemblance."

Arjun examined the photo closely. "Yeah, it does look like him. But what about the sixth photo?"

The room fell silent as they turned their attention to the last photo. Despite their best efforts, it remained a mystery. The image was completely undeveloped, a blank space, due to the glow of the fire which might have gotten in-front of the camera while the picture was clicked, where the face should have been. It was as if the photo itself was refusing to give up its secrets.

"Why can't we develop this one?" Maya asked, frustration evident in her voice.

The IT specialist shrugged. "We've tried everything. It's like there's nothing there to develop."

Arjun's eyes narrowed. "We can't just leave it at that. There has to be an explanation."

"Also, we have the AI-aged photo of the girl," Manoj said, bringing up the image on the screen. The girl's face appeared, aged to show what she might look like now. It was a haunting image, her green eyes seeming to hold secrets of their own.

"We need to visit Allookkara again, tomorrow early morning we start at 7:30 sharp," Arjun said, determination in his voice. "We need to find out more about the girl and any connections she might have."

The team exchanged glances, their resolve strengthening. "Agreed," Arjun continued. "We can't ignore any lead, no matter how small."

"We'll prepare for the trip," Manoj said. "Gather all the information we have and be ready to move out."

Arjun nodded. "This time, we need to be thorough. We can't afford to miss anything."

With a renewed sense of purpose, they began their preparations, each member of the team driven by the need to uncover the truth. The mystery of the undeveloped photo and the girl's identity weighed heavily on their minds as they readied themselves for their next journey to Allookkara, hoping to uncover the final pieces of the puzzle.

Arjun and Manoj had to go and meet DIG to update him about the findings. They had to wait for a long time as DIG was summoned by the Minister for an urgent meeting. And the meeting with DIG didn't go well for them as he was expecting this to be finished much earlier.

On the drive back, Arjun felt bad that he refused the coffee with Kavitha, remembering the slight disappointment in her eyes when he declined. His rationale to himself was that he started to understand that she was developing closeness with him but he couldn't take any move which he considered as cheating Divya. But she has been so helpful and instrumental in this case and hence he wanted to keep her happy.

He clenched the steering wheel tighter, conflicted. Keeping Kavitha happy mattered to him, and she'd played such a pivotal role in their search for answers. It felt wrong to push her away. On an impulse, he pulled out his phone, thumb hovering over her number for a moment before he pressed 'call.'

"Arjun?" Her voice was bright, a little surprised.

"So," he said, forcing a casual tone, "about that coffee... Where are we meeting?"

There was a brief pause, and he could almost hear her smile on the other end of the line. "How about the café near the Marine drive? The one with the terrace view?"

"Sounds perfect. I'll be there in half an hour," he said, his heart beating faster.

•••

Kavitha was waiting on the terrace when Arjun arrived, sunlight catching in her hair. She smiled as he sat down. "Glad you changed your mind. I was starting to think you are avoiding me."

"Just had a lot on my mind," he said, his tone softer than he intended.

They talked, first about the case, then more personal things. The conversation grew quieter, more intimate. Kavitha's expression softened. "You know, Arjun... I couldn't have done any of this without you."

Arjun felt a pang of emotion but pushed it down. He couldn't let himself go there. "We do make a good team," he said, the words heavy with unspoken meaning.

She gave him a sad smile, seeming to understand his hesitation. "Yeah. We do."

They shifted back to the case. "It's been two days since we crossed over to Mohit's & Neeta's universe," Kavitha said, concern creeping into her voice. "We need to check on what the detective agency has found for us."

"Yes, Kavitha. I think I have recovered and am ready to do it again. Let's plan to do the travel tomorrow night" Arjun said in agreement.

They spent some more time together and then left the café.

Just before dropping Kavitha in front of her villa, Arjun informed her about their impending visit to Allookkara. "We're going back to Allookkara tomorrow morning," he said, his voice filled with determination. "We need to follow up on these new leads."

Kavitha's eyes lit up with determination. "I want to join," she said firmly. "We need to get to the bottom of this together."

CHAPTER 15

THE JOURNEY TO ALLOOKKARA

The team—Arjun, Manoj, Rajiv, Maya, and Kavitha—prepared for their journey. With the photo of the girl in hand, they set off towards Allookkara, the remote village that had become the focal point of their investigation. The trip was long, the road winding through dense forests and rugged terrain.

Upon arriving in Allookkara, they were greeted by the local guide Rajan whom Rajiv had found on his previous visit. The guide, an older man with a weathered face and knowing eyes, greeted them with a nod. "Welcome back," he said. "I hear you're looking for more answers."

"We are," Arjun replied. "We need to go deeper into the jungle, where the rituals are performed. We have a photo of a girl we need to inquire about."

The guide's expression darkened slightly. "It's a dangerous area," he warned. "The people there don't take kindly to outsiders asking questions. But as you are insisting, I'll take you. But anything and everything is at your own risk."

The group followed the guide through the dense jungle, the canopy above blocking out much of the sunlight. The air was thick and humid, and the sounds of wildlife echoed around them. After a long trek, they reached a clearing where a group of priest-like figures were gathered, performing rituals around a sacred fire.

Arjun approached cautiously, holding up the photo of the girl. "Excuse me, we're from the police department and we're looking for information about this girl," he said.

The priests turned to face them, their expressions hardening. One of them, an elderly man with a long white beard, stepped forward. "Why do you seek information about her?" he demanded.

"We believe she's connected to our investigation," Arjun explained. "We need to know what happened to her."

The priest's eyes narrowed. "She is a spirit now," he said cryptically. "Her story is not for you to know."

Before Arjun could press further, the atmosphere changed dramatically. The priests began to chant louder, their voices rising in anger. The group sensed the shift and prepared to retreat, but it was too late. The priests advanced aggressively, and chaos ensued.

In the scramble to escape, Rajan was struck by a dart, and immediately he felt a burning sensation spread through his body. The group managed to break free and fled through the jungle, the priests' angry shouts echoing behind them. They made it back to their vehicle, but Rajan was in bad shape.

"We need to get him to a hospital, NOW!" Kavitha shouted, panic in her voice.

They drove as fast as they could to the nearest hospital. Rajan's condition worsened rapidly, his breathing becoming labored. They arrived just in time, and the doctors immediately took him in for treatment. Arjun and the rest of the team waited anxiously; their hearts heavy with worry.

Hours later, a doctor emerged, his expression serious. "He's stable now," he said. "It was a close call. The poison was potent, but we managed to neutralize it."

Relief washed over the team. Manoj, always the pragmatic one, took a sample of Rajan's blood containing the poison and instructed Maya to send it to Dr. Varma for analysis. "We need to know what we're dealing with," he said grimly.

Meanwhile, the local guide had an idea. "There's someone I know who might be able to help," he said. "He's a friend of the priests, but he's not like them. He might be willing to talk."

The team, intrigued and eager to uncover the truth, but with the guide in no condition to take them, asks his brother, Bala to guide them to this mysterious helper. Bala, whose reputation for wisdom and deep knowledge of local lore was unmatched, lent credibility to Arjun's words and intentions.

As they moved deeper into the village, the surroundings began to change. The bustling market and familiar sights gave way to narrower, winding paths flanked by ancient trees and small, weathered houses. The air grew heavier with the scent of earth and foliage, and a palpable sense of history enveloped them. Every step seemed to echo the stories and secrets of the past.

Finally, they arrived at a small, humble home at the edge of the village. It stood modestly, with its thatched roof and clay walls, blending seamlessly into the natural landscape. Despite its simplicity, the house exuded an aura of tranquility and wisdom, as if it had witnessed countless tales and held many secrets within its walls.

An old man, frail but with eyes that sparkled with sharp intelligence, greeted them at the door. His presence commanded respect, and his gaze seemed to penetrate beyond the physical, seeing into their very souls. Bala stepped forward, introducing the old man with a tone of reverence.

"This is Raghavan," Bala said. "He used to be a helper to the ritual priests many years ago."

Raghavan nodded slightly, acknowledging his past with a hint of melancholy. His face, lined with the marks of time, softened as he regarded the team. It was clear that he held a deep connection to the village's history and the mysteries they sought to unravel.

"We need your help," Arjun said, showing him the photo of the girl. "Do you recognize her?"

The old man examined the photo carefully for some time. The expression on his face slowly transformed from curiosity to scared. "Yes," he said finally. "I remember her. It was a long time ago. She died during a ritual. It was a tragic accident, the only one I've ever seen."

"Can you tell us more about her?" Kavitha asked gently.

"She was an orphan," the old man said, his voice tinged with sadness. "No family, no one to remember her but us. She had slightly green-colored eyes, a rare sight here."

Arjun felt a chill run down his spine. "What happened during the ritual?"

"It was a one-time accident," the old man explained. "The priests were conducting a powerful ceremony, and something went wrong. A sword pierced through her. She died that night, and ever since, her spirit is said to haunt these parts."

As they prepared to leave, the old man called them back. "Wait," he said. "There's something else. The priest who conducted the ritual that night was found dead about a year later, under suspicious circumstances. Many believe it was the girl's spirit seeking revenge."

The revelation hung heavy in the air. The team thanked the old man and headed back to their vehicle, their minds racing with new questions and possibilities.

"We need to get to the bottom of this," Arjun said, determination in his voice. "We're closer than ever to understanding what happened, but we need more information."

As they drove back to their base, the car was filled with a heavy silence. Each team member was lost in thought, grappling with the strange and tragic events they had uncovered. Just like the evening darkness that was becoming thicker outside, the enigma of the undeveloped photo and the girl's identity loomed large in their minds, driving them with a renewed urgency to find the truth. They dispersed on reaching the station, where everyone went to take rest after an eventful long day, but Arjun and Kavitha rushed to her villa. Both of them had another greater plan in their mind, the travel to their alternate selves, Mohit & Neeta, after a gap of 2 days.

CHAPTER 16

THE TURNING POINT

Arjun's eyes fluttered open, the dim light of dawn filtering through unfamiliar curtains. He felt a strange warmth beside him and turned to see Kavitha lying close, her breathing soft and rhythmic. The surroundings were not immediately recognizable, and a surge of confusion washed over him. This wasn't his room in fact it wasn't even Mohit's room.

He glanced around, trying to gather his bearings. The room was cozy, and decorated with a mix of modern and traditional elements. It was then that he realized they were in Neeta's apartment. His heart raced as he recalled the events of the previous night.

Kavitha stirred and opened her eyes, meeting Arjun's gaze. Instead of the embarrassment he expected, she smiled softly. "Good morning," she said, her voice gentle and warm.

Arjun felt a flush of heat rise to his cheeks. "Good morning," he replied, trying to keep his voice steady. "This is... unexpected."

Kavitha sat up, adjusting the blanket around her. "It is, but I've been thinking. Maybe this isn't so bad. Maybe it's an opportunity to understand things better." Her tone was contemplative, hinting at the growing bond between them.

Arjun nodded, trying to focus on the task at hand. "We need to figure out why we're here. Either Mohit and Neeta have become closer because of the rumors, or the rumors started because they got close."

Their discussion was interrupted by the ringing of Mohit's phone. He answered, hearing the angry voice of the accountant at the detective agency on the other end. They were furious due to Mohit's lack of response the previous day. Arjun realized that they spoke to the actual personality of Mohit, who was not aware of any of these.

"We were about to halt all operations, Mr. Mohit," the finance guy from the agency said, his tone sharp. "We need assurance of payment before proceeding with any further steps."

Taking a deep breath, Arjun composed himself and replied in a calm, measured voice, "I apologize for the inconvenience. This is Mohit. I was not well for a couple of days and was almost out of my senses. I'll arrange the full payment immediately."

The agency representative, reassured by the promise of payment, informed Andrew that the financial hold had been lifted. At Arjun's request, he patched the call through to Andrew. Andrew informed that the investigation has been completed and he is ready with the final reports. They agreed to meet at Mohit's office by 9:30.

Arjun and Kavitha barely had time to catch their breath—they got fresh immediately and grabbed a quick coffee & a bite at a nearby shop before hurrying to Mohit's office. Once there, Arjun immediately took out the cheque book of Mohit, wrote the balance amount for Blackstone Investigations and dispatched it through the messenger. The amount which is being given is big. He couldn't imagine how Mohit was going to handle this when he comes to know about this much amount being transferred. Or maybe this is peanuts for him.

Then, they waited anxiously, the minutes dragging by. Every tick of the clock seemed louder. Finally, at exactly 09:30, Andrew walked in.

He greeted both of them with the same emotionless facial expression. Then, without acknowledging the financial drama, he launched directly into his findings. "We've identified six key connections among the six individuals you mentioned," he said, laying out a series of printed documents on the table.

"First, there's Munna—the guy who runs the karak tea stand at the popular tea shop in Mamzar, Dubai. All six of our subjects visit the shop regularly. Munna is from Kerala."

Arjun's brow furrowed, but he didn't interrupt as Andrew continued.

"Second," Andrew said, pointing to a photo of a couple, "Marlon and Jennifer. They're a married couple, both working as insurance agents at Lifeline Life Insurance Company. They handle all six individuals as clients, often doing joint sales calls and follow-ups. They're originally from the Philippines."

Arjun and Kavitha exchanged a quick glance, noting the coincidence. Andrew moved on.

"Third connection is Akram Waqas," Andrew said, emphasizing the name. "He's a messenger at Lifeline Life Insurance Company. He's responsible for collecting monthly or quarterly insurance premiums from four of the six, excluding Jasmin and Munna. However, he also visits the massage center where Jasmin works to pick up the owner's payment. On top of that, Akram runs a small illegal chit fund on the side—Jasmin and Munna are both participants."

Arjun leaned forward, the picture becoming clearer, but there was more.

"The fourth link involves banking," Andrew said, tapping another file. "All of them, except Jasmin, have accounts at the same bank—Continental Bank of Dubai. Even more specifically, all of their accounts are managed by the same relationship manager, Jaison. Incidentally, Jaison is a regular customer at the massage center where Jasmin works."

Andrew paused, his voice lowering slightly. "And finally, they all see the same doctor—Dr. Amani Sleiman. She's a well-known internal medicine specialist at Jumeirah Town Hospital, and she also works at a few clinics within that hospital group. She does monthly outreach at the labor camp where Jasmin stays, providing free medical check-ups, and that's how she knows Jasmin."

Arjun took a deep breath, absorbing the implications. "So, they're all linked—through tea shops, insurance, banking, and medical care. It's like a web."

Andrew nodded, gathering the documents from the table and sliding them into a neat folder before handing the entire file to Kavitha. His manner was brisk, almost rehearsed, as he delivered his closing statement. "I assume you're satisfied with the investigation results. You got what you were looking for," he said, extending his hand for a firm handshake with Arjun, and then with Kavitha. "As per our contract agreement, this assignment is officially over. And as per the confidentiality agreement signed, we won't communicate anything about this investigation further unless you initiate a new assignment. I hope that's clear. It's been a pleasure working with you both, and feel free to reach out if you need us again. Thank you."

Without another word, he left the room, his departure as swift and professional as the rest of the meeting. Arjun and Kavitha stood there for a few moments, staring at the closed door, processing the finality of it all.

They settled back at the desk, spreading out the photos and documents in front of them. It felt like the room had suddenly become quieter, the weight of what they had uncovered settling around them. Kavitha was silent, studying the photos intently, her eyes narrowing as she absorbed the details. Arjun could tell she was memorizing each face, embedding them into her mind.

"This is huge," Kavitha said, finally breaking the silence. "I think this is the biggest breakthrough we've had using our alternate universe method. We've identified the alternate versions of six suspects in this universe. We're so close."

Arjun nodded but raised a finger to correct her. "Not six," he said. "Four."

Kavitha looked confused; her brow furrowed.

"Remember," Arjun said, leaning forward, "we have proof that the killer is male in our universe. That means we can rule out two of them—Jennifer, the insurance agent, and Dr. Amani Sleiman. So, we're down to four possibilities."

Kavitha's expression cleared, and she nodded slowly. "Good point. That does narrow it down," she said, a hint of relief in her voice. "It makes things more manageable."

They spent the next few hours strategizing, carefully piecing together how to use the information in their own universe. They had a clearer path now, but there were still gaps to fill.

By the time they left the office, it was nearly 1:30 PM. They stopped at a quiet restaurant nearby, ordering a late lunch. As they waited for their food, Kavitha leaned back in her chair, thoughtfully stirring her coffee. "It would make things so much simpler if we could identify any recent behavioral changes in the alternate versions of our 6 victims towards those four common connections," she said.

Arjun raised an eyebrow. "Why would that help?"

Kavitha's eyes brightened, and she launched into an explanation. "Remember what I told you during our second meeting? If someone is murdered in one universe, the killer's and victim's alternate selves often exhibit subtle behavioral shifts in the other universes—fear, hostility, avoidance. In this case, we have one killer and multiple victims. If we can find evidence of these changes in behavior—recent ones— between the 6 persons and any one of the 4, we might be able to pinpoint which of the four is our target. Then, we just need to identify that one person's alternate personality in our universe. Case solved."

Arjun's eyes widened in realization. "You're right," he said. "How did I not think of that? It's exactly the clue we need."

Kavitha smiled, pleased with herself, but she remained cautious. "But the problem is how. We need to detect these changes in each of the alternate personalities of the victims, and that's going to take time. And we don't have a clear way of extracting that information."

Arjun smiled; his expression ignited by a sudden surge of determination. "I think we need to bring in Blackstone and Andrew again. Maybe they can get this done."

Before Kavitha could respond, Arjun pulled out his phone and dialed Andrew's number. Andrew picked up after the second ring. "Mohit?" he said, his voice professional and guarded.

"Andrew, I need another favor," Arjun said without preamble. "I need to know if there have been any behavioral changes—recent ones—towards these four individuals: Munna, Marlon, Akram, and Jaison, from the six other people involved. We've only got 24 hours to get this done. Do you have resources who can handle this?"

Andrew paused for a moment, then answered, "We can do it. But, as I said before, this will be a new assignment. The payment will be higher due to the time constraints, and this time we'll need full payment upfront. I'll send the invoice and digital agreement to your email—sign it, pay, and we'll have the report ready maximum by tomorrow evening."

Arjun felt contended and replied sternly," Agreed, don't worry about the payment. It will be done upfront. But are you sure you can do it in such a short time? And how?"

This time, Andrew's tone hardened, "I think you need the information and you will get it. We take up a case only when we know that we can do it and how we do it, that's our problem. You don't have to worry about that. Hope I have made myself clear. Take care and bye Mohit".

The call ended abruptly, leaving Arjun holding the phone, feeling both confident and anxious. He turned to Kavitha, who was watching him closely. "It's settled," he said. "They'll get the information. We just need to make sure the payment is ready."

Kavitha nodded, relief softening her features. "Let's head back to the office and get it done," she said.

They went back to Mohit's office, arranged for the payment to be processed, and finalized the paperwork. By the time they were finished, the sun was already setting. They split up, each heading back to their respective apartments, both focused on preparing for another night's travel to their own universe.

They had so much to get done there, with this breakthrough.

•••

In their original universe, Kavitha sat at her desk, sketching the faces of the four individuals from her memory. Her artistic skills brought the faces to life on paper, capturing their essence with remarkable accuracy. Seeing the drawings, Arjun felt like they have brought the photos of the 4 people from the other side.

Arjun called his team and Manoj for an urgent meeting in the morning at the tech team's lab at 10:00 AM. He then messaged Manoj to reach his office early by around 9.

Before the team joined, Arjun showed the pictures of the 4 people to Manoj and explained how they had been identified. Manoj was just out of the world hearing this breakthrough.

Shortly Rajiv and Maya came in and they all proceeded to the tech lab.

Arjun placed the copies of the drawings in front of them, "Here they are," he said, placing them on the table. "These are the four people we need to find."

Manoj, turning to the tech team, said, "We need to locate these individuals using the Aadhaar database. It's crucial we find them as soon as possible "

The tech team nodded and set to work, their fingers flying over keyboards as they began the search. Maya and Rajiv exchanged puzzled glances.

"How did you get these pictures?" Maya asked, suspicion lacing her voice

Arjun and Manoj shared a quick look. "We have our sources," Arjun said smoothly, deflecting the question. "What's important is finding these people and understanding their connection to the case."

Rajiv seemed about to press further, but a sharp glance from Manoj silenced him. The team turned their attention back to the task at hand, the room filled with the hum of technology and the scent of coffee.

As they were eagerly waiting for the results from the tech team, Dr. Varma arrived with a stack of reports. His expression was grave as he addressed the team. "I've analyzed the poison found in Rajan's system and compared it to the poison from the victims. They are different."

The team absorbed this information, their minds working to fit this new piece into the puzzle. "But this poison doesn't match so it has nothing to do with the murders, right?" Manoj mused.

"Probably not, as it seems to be a wrong lead. But anyway, we were able to remove that suspicion." Dr. Varma said before leaving.

By afternoon, the tech team returned with their findings. The room was dimly lit, the glow from computer screens casting eerie shadows on the walls. The air was thick with anticipation.

"We've located the four individuals," the lead technician announced. "Here are their details. "

One is Joseph Antony. He is settled in a place called Kothamangalam in Ernakulam District.

Second is Adarsh S. He is from Thriuvalla in Pathanamthitta District.

Third one is Adel Farhan, and he is from Calicut district.

And the fourth one Aneesh Madhav, basically from Kottayam District but working in Bangalore.

Arjun and Manoj scanned the information, adrenaline rushing as they realized how close they were getting. "This is solid work," Arjun said, taking a deep breath. "We need a deep dive on these people—full background checks. Activities, travel, communications, web searches, mobile locations—everything from the past six months.

This has to be our top priority."

Manoj instructed Rajiv and Maya to take care of this. Noticing the frustration in their expressions, he added, "We're getting closer. We need to stay together, focused, and be prepared for whatever we uncover."

The team scattered to begin their tasks, but Arjun and Manoj remained behind, sharing a moment of silent understanding. Manoj broke the silence with a smile. "How about a beer at The Black Rock?" he suggested. "Your favorite spot."

Arjun hesitated, tempted, but shook his head. "I can't," he said. "I need to do the travel to the other side to get to the bottom of this. Let's save the celebration for when this is all over."

Their session was interrupted by a shocking phone call. Another murder had been reported, identical in style to the previous ones. This time the victim is Vijay Samuel, a prominent businessman and the murder occurred early morning by around 01:00 AM.

Arjun's heart sank as he heard the news. "Another one?" he muttered; his voice laced with frustration.

Manoj slammed his fist on the desk, frustration and determination mingling in his expression. " We need to act fast. We need to catch this guy before he strikes again. The city's on edge, and people are scared. Killer's making a mockery of us, flaunting his twisted game right under our noses."

Rajiv and Maya came rushing into the room, their faces mirroring the same mixture of shock and dread. It felt as if the killer was always one step ahead, taunting them with each new crime.

The news of Vijay's murder spread like wildfire, tightening the noose of panic around the city's neck, with crowds gathering outside police stations and reporters swarming the crime scene. Within hours, the news of Vijay's brutal death exploded across the media, sending shockwaves through the city. Headlines blared the details: "One more murder in the 'Past & Future Serial Killer case'.

Prominent Businessman Murdered in Chilling Copycat Crime." Grim-faced anchors dissected the incident, debating theories and sensationalizing every gruesome detail.

The pressure on the investigation team grew unbearable, and every failure was magnified in the public eye. The team assembled, faces grim and set, knowing the clock was ticking louder than ever. Manoj asked Rajiv and Maya to rush to the murder site to collect the details and to do an investigation from their end.

Arjun's phone rang as if it's an alarm for them to wake up once again. The DIG, a man known for his stern demeanor and rigid expectations, convened with Arjun and Manoj at the police headquarters. The atmosphere was tense as soon as the three met at the conference room, the weight of the city's unrest hanging heavily between them.

The DIG wasted no time in expressing his frustrations. His voice, usually composed and authoritative, carried a sharp edge of impatience. "Arjun and Manoj, this investigation has been dragging for far too long," he began, his tone brooking no argument. "The public is restless, the press is on our backs, and here we are, seemingly no closer to catching this killer. What's going on?"

Arjun, feeling the strain of sleepless nights and continuous pressure, responded with a firmness that matched the DIG's intensity. "We're closer than ever before," he asserted, standing his ground. "We've prepared the final list of suspects and we are just a small distance away from finding the killer. I just need a bit more time."

The DIG slammed his hand down on the table, making his displeasure unmistakably clear. "Time is a luxury we don't have, Arjun!" he barked. "I'm giving you five days—five days to bring me results, or I'll have to take drastic measures."

The room charged with a palpable tension as Arjun met the DIG's gaze, his resolve hardening. "Thank you, sir. Five days is more than enough for us," Arjun replied, his voice steady despite the turmoil brewing within. "We will catch him. I promise you that."

Their eyes locked in a moment of silent confrontation, each man gauging the other's determination. Finally, the DIG nodded curtly, the briefest acknowledgment of Arjun's commitment. "Make sure you keep that promise," he warned as he turned to leave, his steps echoing in the nearly empty room.

As the door closed behind the DIG, Arjun exhaled slowly, the encounter adding another layer of urgency to their mission. The confrontation, though uncomfortable, galvanized him; he knew there was no room for error. The next five days would be crucial, not just for the investigation, but for the safety of the entire city. The stakes were higher than ever, and failure was not an option.

Arjun and Manoj returned to the station, their stride purposeful, their mind already racing with plans. By evening, Rajiv and Maya joined them at the conference room, with the reports on the latest murder. According to the report, Vijay Samuel, 58 years, had died while enjoying a drink at one of his regular pubs. Witnesses said he was talking with friends when he suddenly collapsed, gasping for air. An ambulance rushed him to the hospital, but the doctor confirmed he was already dead on arrival. The initial cause of death was listed as a heart attack, just like the previous cases.

The real twist came the following morning. While the pub staff cleaned the floor, one of them discovered a small, folded note from under Vijay's table. The message was chillingly familiar: "Payback for your past, from my future." That discovery shifted the narrative—the seemingly natural death was reclassified as another act by the notorious 'Past & Future' serial killer.

"We have five days," Manoj announced to the group, who looked back at him with a mix of anxiety and determination. "Let's use every second. It's time to end this."

They parted ways—Manoj heading home, and Arjun back to Kavitha's villa, steeling himself for the next step.

CHAPTER 17

THE FINAL STEP

Arjun arrived at Kavitha's villa that evening, his mood dark and unsettled. A call from Divya on the way had provided some comfort, but the pressure of the investigation was grinding him down, his frustration mounting with each dead end. The latest murder weighed heavily on him, tightening the knot of urgency in his chest.

Kavitha wasn't faring much better, but she had pushed past the emotion and focused on the next step. She had already mapped out a plan for their mission in the other universe and was waiting for Arjun to arrive so they could go over it before making their travel tonight.

The moment he stepped through the door; Kavitha didn't waste a second. "Arjun, I have a plan," she said, skipping any small talk. "Andrew's already working on tracking behavioral shifts between the alternate versions of the six victims and our four suspects. But I think we need to move faster.

Arjun's eyes sharpened, and Kavitha pressed on. "As soon as we cross over, I'm going to sketch Vijay Samuel's face. Then we'll visit each of the four suspects and watch their reactions. The murder happened just this morning in our universe which means the impact would have started since the previous night there—the changes in behavior should be fresh, obvious. Whoever confirms this behavioral transformation from or towards Vijay's alternate version will be our guy."

Her confidence was steady, and Arjun found himself nodding, the urgency of the plan driving away his exhaustion. “If the shift is as dramatic as you think, we’ll know exactly who we’re looking for,” he said, determination settling into his features.

“One of them will show their hand,” Kavitha said firmly. “And when they do, we’ll have our killer.”

Arjun nodded without looking up. “We don’t have the luxury of time,” he replied, his voice carrying a weight that underscored the gravity of their mission. “Let’s make sure we come back with answers today.”

As the sky darkened, they prepared for the transition, gathering the materials they needed and checking over the notes they had compiled. They moved with a quiet efficiency, the silence between them underscored by a shared determination.

Shortly, Arjun and Kavitha experienced a familiar sensation that signaled the transition to the alternate universe. The world around them blurred and shifted, and they found themselves back in Mohit’s and Neeta’s world.

As soon as he woke up as Mohit, Arjun got ready and left home early without seeing anyone, picked up Kavitha, and they headed straight to the Gupta Regal Empire building. They were barely through the entrance when Shagufta, the receptionist, greeted them with a bright smile. “Good morning, both of you,” she said. Then, lowering her voice, she leaned closer to Arjun. “Hey, Mohit, just a heads up—Mr. Gupta seemed really upset this morning. I heard, quietly, that he’s asked the finance department to review your recent transactions. I’m pretty sure he’ll want to speak with you soon.”

Arjun’s heart skipped a beat, and he shot a quick glance at Kavitha, as both knew the reason. Arjun felt a feeling of guilt but he had no time for a confrontation with Mohit’s father today. “Thanks for the warning,” he murmured, giving Shagufta a tight smile. He and Kavitha exchanged a knowing look and quickly slipped out of the building. They had no time for a confrontation.

They found a quiet café nearby and settled into a corner table. Kavitha wasted no time, grabbing her sketchbook and beginning to sketch Vijay Samuel's face. Arjun watched her with a mix of awe and familiarity; he was used to her skill by now, but each time she finished a portrait, he couldn't help but be amazed. As she added the final strokes, the image of Vijay Samuel came to life on the page with striking clarity.

"Every time," Arjun said, shaking his head with admiration. "You never cease to amaze me."

Kavitha looked up and gave him a small smile.

"Let's hope this one helps us catch the killer. As planned, let's start meeting the four; one by one, and find our guy" she said, handing over the drawing to him. "We're getting closer Arjun. I can feel it", She said.

Arjun nodded, his mind already mapping out the next steps today. As they strategized, the enormity of their task loomed large. The stakes were higher than ever, and every second counted. " Munna, Jaison, Akram, and Marlon; Who should we start with?", asked Arjun.

They decided to begin with Marlon, approaching him under the guise of being a prospective client interested in an insurance policy. Kavitha called him as Neeta, the secretary of Mohit Gupta, and asked for a meeting. Marlon was quite excited and confirmed for the meeting at M-Café in Dubai Mall for 1:30 PM, as he was already on his way to meet a client.

With time before the meeting, they proceeded to meet Munna, from whom, they thought it was easiest to extract information.

They arrived at the café. It had only a handful of customers as it was morning time. A middle-aged man with a kind demeanor greeted them with a warm smile. Arjun asked for Munna. The man nodded and stepped back to call for Munna. Shortly, Munna approached their table, his friendly demeanor instantly putting them at ease. After ordering tea, they gestured for him to join them, but Munna remained standing nearby.

"Hello, sir and madam," Munna said, his eyes twinkling. "You're friends of Shafna Madam, right?"

"Yes, Munna," Arjun began cautiously. "We need your help. Can you look at this picture and tell us if you recognize this person?" He slid showing the photo of the sketch of Vijay Samuel on his phone.

Munna's face lit up with recognition, and he nodded eagerly. "Of course! This is Ahmed Sir. He's a big shot and a very kind man. He comes here often for tea and always leaves a generous tip. He just left after his regular morning visit."

"That's great, Munna," Kavitha said. "But tell me, did he seem different today? Anything unusual in how he behaved with you?"

Munna frowned slightly, shaking his head. "No, madam, not at all. He was the same as always—kind and polite. Look," he added with a proud smile, "he even told me to keep the balance of 3 dirhams as a tip."

Kavitha glanced at Arjun, subtly signaling that this wasn't their suspect. They finished their tea and left the café, setting their sights on the next name on their list: Akram. They were anticipating a positive outcome from that meeting.

Using the pretext of selling a car, Arjun and Kavitha contacted Akram, knowing his reputation for taking up any deal for money. As expected, he immediately agreed to meet them within 45 minutes at a parking lot near Karama Centre.

When Akram arrived, he immediately began inspecting the car. As he examined it, he asked, "Where did you get my number?"

Arjun, maintaining his cover, casually said, "Ahmed referred us." When Akram appeared confused, Arjun pulled out his phone and showed him the photo of Vijay.

Akram's reaction was one of mild surprise.

For a brief moment, Arjun and Kavitha felt like they might be onto something, but the hope quickly faded.

Akram said, "That's Mr. Ahmed Hamza. I've done some deliveries and cheque pick-up at his office, but we've barely spoken. Honestly, I didn't think he even knew me." Akram's surprise was genuine—there was no sign of any significant connection or behavioral shift.

Arjun and Kavitha understood that this was not the person. They gave some random excuse and got rid of Akram, as they had to continue their search.

As they drove toward Dubai Mall, Arjun's frustration bubbled over. "Are you sure this theory is solid?" he asked Kavitha, his doubt evident.

Kavitha met his gaze, her voice steady despite her own creeping uncertainty. "I'm 100% sure, Arjun. We still have two more suspects to go. We'll find it today." But deep down, she felt the weight of her own fears—what if her theory might be wrong after all?

As planned, Arjun and Kavitha arrived at M-Café around 1:15 PM and waited for Marlon. At exactly 1:30, Marlon walked in with his wife cum colleague, Jennifer. Both of them lit up with excitement upon seeing Mohit Gupta, clearly eager to impress such a high-profile client.

Kavitha introduced herself smoothly as Neeta, Mohit's secretary, and explained that they were looking for the best insurance plan for him. Sensing an opportunity, Marlon and Jennifer immediately launched into pitching high-value policies, each endorsing the other for their recommendations.

The discussion carried on for a while, with Marlon guiding the conversation. At one point, Kavitha excused herself to visit the washroom, and Jennifer offered to accompany her. The two women left the table, leaving Arjun alone with Marlon.

Seizing the opportunity, Arjun leaned forward with a friendly smile. "You've been giving us great advice. Thanks for that. I can see why you'd leave such a strong impression on your clients—probably why Ahmed recommended you. You know him well, right? His full name is Ahmed Hamza. He spoke very highly of you both."

Marlon frowned slightly; his confusion evident. "Ahmed Hamza?" he repeated. "I can't recall anyone by that name to whom I have sold any recently."

Arjun quickly pulled out his phone and showed Marlon the sketch of Vijay Samuel. "This is Ahmed. Does this ring a bell?"

Marlon studied the image, then shook his head. "I don't think so," he said apologetically. "But I'll check my older files just in case." He snapped a photo of the sketch on Arjun's phone for reference.

By the time Kavitha and Jennifer returned to the table, it was clear to Arjun that Marlon wasn't their suspect. He exchanged a quick glance with Kavitha, subtly signaling another dead end.

They wrapped up the meeting by signing an application for a policy and promised to arrange for the premium payment within the next day. As they left M-Café around 3:45 PM, the weight of yet another disappointment hung heavily over them, but they knew they couldn't give up yet.

On their way to meet the final person on their list—Jaison—Arjun and Kavitha sat in tense silence, knowing this could be their last chance. Either Jaison was the key, or another dead end awaited them. Their emotions were a mix of cautious excitement and mounting dread.

As they were about to start the car, Arjun's phone rang. It was Andrew. "Hey, Mohit," Andrew said. "We've completed the assignment. I can meet you with the report whenever you're ready."

"That's great, Andrew," Arjun replied. "But can you give me a quick summary now? If there's anything significant, just send the full report to my email."

"Understood," Andrew said. "Here's the short version: we didn't find any recent behavioral changes among the individuals you mentioned. I'll email you the detailed report shortly, but that's the gist of it. Hope it helps. It's been a pleasure working with you both once again, and feel free to reach out if you need us again. Thank you."

Andrew disconnected the call, leaving a heavy silence in the car. Kavitha exhaled slowly; her unease evident. "This feels like a bad omen," she muttered. "Nothing's gone right today. But we can't stop." Both knew that they needed the answer today and they were quite confident in finding it out.

For Jaison, they used the same approach as with Marlon and Akram. Posing as representatives of Mohit's fabricated startup, Kavitha called and requested an urgent meeting to discuss opening a new business account. Hearing Mohit Gupta's name, Jaison agreed immediately, setting the meeting for 6:00 PM at a coffee shop in DIFC.

During the meeting, following the same modus operandi, Kavitha smoothly introduced Ahmed as their supposed referrer and showed Jaison the sketch of Vijay. Both she and Arjun studied Jaison's expression intently, hoping for a telltale reaction. But to their dismay, his face remained neutral—not the response they were hoping for. It was like he had never seen this guy.

"I'm sorry," Jaison said, studying the sketch. "I don't recognize this man. He might be a connection to one of my customers, but I'm certain I don't know him."

The words hit Arjun and Kavitha like a blow. They exchanged a glance, their expressions reflecting their growing despair. Another dead end. Their last lead was gone, and the weight of failure settled heavily over them. For the first time, they were unsure what to do next.

The drive back to Neeta's apartment was steeped in silence. Arjun gripped the steering wheel tightly, his mind racing with self-doubt. Had he been wrong to rely so heavily on this method? All the time and effort they'd poured into this investigation felt wasted, the dead ends weighing heavily on his shoulders.

Beside him, Kavitha stared out the window, her own thoughts mirroring his. She felt a deep ache of disappointment, questioning whether her research and theories had failed. Yet, somewhere in the back of her mind, a nagging feeling persisted—a sense that they were missing something crucial, that the answer was still within reach.

Kavitha broke the silence, her voice thoughtful yet tinged with frustration. "Arjun, I think something went wrong—somewhere. I don't believe the theory is flawed, but we've missed something. I just don't know what."

Arjun nodded; his brow furrowed in agreement. "I've been thinking the same. But the problem is, we're running out of time to figure it out. We don't even know what we missed, let alone how to retrace our steps to fix it. I can't even—"

His words were cut short by the sharp ring of his phone. Kavitha picked it up and glanced at the screen. "It's Marlon," she said.

"Just ignore it," Arjun muttered, assuming it was about the insurance policy.

But Kavitha hesitated, then shook her head. "No, we should take it." Before Arjun could object, she answered the call, connecting it to the car's Bluetooth system.

Marlon's voice crackled through the speaker, packed with excitement. "Hi, Mr. Mohit! I mentioned Mr. Ahmed and showed the picture I took from you, to my wife Jennifer. And she recognized him immediately. I'll hand the phone to her—she can explain."

Jennifer took over, her tone eager and deferential. "That's Mr. Ahmed, a big shot, just like you," she began, clearly trying to impress. "I met him ages ago during a cold visit and have been trying to get a follow-up appointment ever since. Honestly, he always seemed irritated—he even shouted at me once."

She paused, her tone shifting to one of disbelief. "But out of nowhere, he called me this morning and asked to meet about a policy. When I met him, he was completely different—polite, even warm. He said he admired my persistence and wanted to take a policy from me. It was like a sudden shift in his character for me. What's more surprising was that he also mentioned referring to his friends. Actually, Marlon hasn't met him yet, that's why he didn't recognize the photo."

Arjun and Kavitha exchanged stunned looks, trying to process what they'd just heard. Confusion and shock clouded their thoughts; this wasn't what they expected.

"Thank you, Marlon and Jennifer," Arjun said, forcing calm into his voice. "You've been incredibly helpful, and we really appreciate the call back. It's great to know about this connection."

He ended the call, still grappling with the implications of what they'd just learned.

As they drove back, conflicting emotions filled the car. On one hand, their hearts raced with excitement—they'd finally found the person linked to the behavioral shift. But confusion lingered; it was Jennifer who had observed the change, a revelation that upended their assumptions. It is a lady, whereas they were expecting it to be a guy.

Kavitha broke the silence, her voice brimming with pride. "See, Arjun? I told you my theory couldn't be wrong. We have our guy—or rather, our 'lady.' Actually, this is revolutionary learning for me too—it proves that alternate personalities of the same person can differ in gender."

She paused, her excitement growing. "Now all we need is to find Jennifer's alternate personality in our universe, and boom, we've got the killer."

Arjun smiled; her enthusiasm infectious. "You're right, Kavitha. I can see where we went wrong now. We were too narrow-minded in our assumptions. But you're also right that this is just the first step. After we find her counterpart, there's still a lot of work to do—finding clues, evidence, and everything we need to make the case stand in the court of law."

The gravity of their task tempered their joy. Before long, they arrived at Neeta's apartment. With quiet determination, they prepared for the return to their own universe. They were almost certain that they were returning from what might be their final trip to this universe. Despite the challenges ahead, they couldn't help but feel a deep sense of accomplishment—their unconventional method had paid off.

CHAPTER 18

THE WEAVE OF FATE

Day 1 after the ultimatum from DIG

Both Arjun and Kavitha woke up at Kavitha's villa. With full of energy, Kavitha immediately got fresh and already started drawing the picture of Jennifer, while sipping her coffee. Arjun kept on watching the way she was bringing a photo copy of Jennifer's face on the paper.

Suddenly, the silence was broken with a call from DIG. He wanted to take an update as of now. Arjun mentioned that he has almost shortlisted the person and will update him very shortly.

Arjun turned to Kavitha and said, "You can complete the drawing and send me an HD photo via email and WhatsApp. I need to get to the station and make the necessary arrangements to take the next steps using it."

Without wasting time, he headed to his apartment to pick up a few essentials before driving straight to the station. On the way, he called Manoj, his voice excited but charged with urgency. "We've got the answer," he said. "But there's still a lot to do. Get the Tech team ready, and make sure Rajiv and Maya are on standby. We'll need everyone focused on what comes next."

At the station, Manoj was waiting in his office, anticipation etched on his face as he prepared to learn the details about the breakthrough Arjun had mentioned. The moment Arjun walked in; Manoj greeted him with a congratulatory hug. "Congratulations! This sounds big," he said, his excitement clear. "The team is already gathered in the conference room."

As they waited to receive the sketch from Kavitha, Arjun briefed Manoj on the key details. He explained how they had pinpointed the individual based on behavioral shifts and shared the startling revelation: in the alternate universe, the killer's counterpart was a woman. Manoj listened intently, his expression shifting between amazement and intrigue. "This sounds like a movie script," he remarked, shaking his head in disbelief.

Just then, Arjun's phone buzzed with a notification—a WhatsApp call from Kavitha. Moments later, another WhatsApp alert popped up. Arjun opened the message, and the detailed sketch of Jennifer appeared on the screen.

He handed the phone to Manoj, who studied the image closely. A slow smile spread across his face, a mix of triumph and determination. "We've got him," Manoj said, his voice steady with confidence.

Immediately, Arjun and Manoj hurried to the conference room, where the entire team was assembled. Arjun didn't want to waste any second. As Arjun projected Jennifer's sketch onto the screen, the room fell silent. Turning to the Tech team, he began, "We've had a major breakthrough." He paused, meeting the eyes of his team. "We've identified the individual we're looking for, and this is the sketch of that person."

The team stared at the screen, clearly taken aback to see a woman's image. They had been working under the assumption, based on evidences collected, that the killer was a man. Arjun and Manoj could feel the unspoken questions brewing among the group.

Sensing the hesitation, Arjun paused, brainstorming on how to explain. Manoj stepped in smoothly, giving him a quick wink before addressing the team. "Our source saw the killer in disguise of a woman," he said with a confident tone. "Which is why the sketch reflects that appearance. The source was able to provide the inputs accordingly only to the sketch artist"

The explanation seemed to satisfy the room. The team members exchanged glances but nodded, accepting the rationale as they refocused on the task ahead.

Turning to the Tech Team, Arjun said urgently, "I need you to work on this sketch and perform a gender transformation. We have to see how the suspect might look without the disguise. Treat this as an emergency—we don't have a moment to lose."

The Tech Team nodded and got to work immediately. Utilizing advanced AI technology, they began generating a gender-swapped version of the sketch under Arjun's watchful eye. The process moved quickly, and within minutes, the software rendered the adjusted image. The result was strikingly lifelike.

"Make the eyes green," Arjun instructed, recalling a specific detail they learned from Asif Ali, the manager of the victim - Dinesh Menon. The team modified it, and the altered image was finalized.

With no time to waste, the completed image, along with the suspect's forensic profile, was distributed to every police station in the region. Simultaneously, under Manoj's instructions, the Tech Team began combing through the Aadhaar database for a match. However, progress was slow—the database wasn't yielding results, likely because the image was sketched and reconstructed rather than an actual photograph.

Realizing the limitations of the search, the team shifted their focus, knowing that their best chance now was for one of the police stations to recognize the suspect and report back. The room hummed with tension as they braced for the next breakthrough.

Hours passed in tense anticipation. The team members were on edge, knowing that time was of the essence. The weight of the case hung heavily in the air; every second feeling more critical than the last. Finally, at around 1:00 PM, the breakthrough arrived. A call came in from a police station in Kothamangalam, a town in Ernakulam District. A constable reported recognizing the man from the altered image.

Manoj immediately asked the operator to connect the call to him, putting the call on speaker so everyone in the room could listen. "Sir," the constable began, his voice steady but with a hint of urgency, "you remember I was instructed to investigate and shadow one Joseph Antony? During my initial visits to his home, I saw this man's photo multiple times—along with Joseph's—in several family pictures on the walls. I also gathered some details during the inquiry."

He continued, "The man in the photo is Vivek James, Joseph Antony's nephew. Vivek's parents passed away when he was a child, and Joseph took him in and raised him. The family is extremely wealthy—generational wealth. Vivek is a college dropout and lives off the family fortune. He doesn't have a steady job and seems to spend his days on his computer and travelling."

As the constable spoke, Arjun was going through the files and piecing things together. His eyes lit up as he made the connection. "Joseph Antony," he said quietly, turning to Manoj, "is Marlon's alternate personality. And Jennifer's alternate personality is closely tied to Marlon. It all adds up now."

Once the constable finished his briefing, Manoj leaned into the call. "Connect me to your station in-charge immediately," he ordered. When the officer came on the line, Manoj issued clear instructions: "Hi Inspector Anand, Arrest Vivek James discreetly and bring him to the Special Investigation Team station in Kochi. Make sure this operation remains low-profile.

Additionally, I'll be dispatching a forensic team to search his residence—please arrange any necessary support for them."

Following this, Arjun directed the forensic team to proceed to Kothamangalam and conduct a thorough search of Vivek's room for any potential evidence.

The team erupted in cheers. After all their efforts, they had finally identified the killer, and an arrest was imminent. The tension that had hung over them for days gave way to palpable excitement and relief. They exchanged smiles and congratulated one another, energized by the breakthrough.

However, in the corner of the room, Rajiv and Maya exchanged uncertain glances. They felt sidelined, unsure of how Arjun and Manoj had managed to pinpoint the killer. The mysterious "source" behind the information puzzled them, but the moment was too charged for them to voice their questions.

Arjun stepped away from the celebration to make a call to the DIG. He gave a concise update on the situation, assuring him, "We've identified the suspect and issued orders for his arrest. I'll keep you informed of any developments."

As Arjun ended the call, the sense of victory in the room was undeniable. The team had finally cracked the case, and soon, the elusive killer would be in custody.

•••

At the police station in Kothamangalam, Inspector Anand's team sprang into action, speeding towards Joseph Antony's residence. The drive was tense, every minute seeming to stretch into eternity. Anand, leading the team, briefed his colleagues on their approach.

"We need to be cautious but quick," he instructed. "We can't afford to let him slip away."

Although Anand hadn't been fully briefed on why Vivek James was a person of interest, he trusted Manoj's orders implicitly. Whatever this case was, it was serious.

When they reached Joseph's residence, disappointment awaited them. Joseph, visibly confused, informed the team that Vivek had left earlier that morning with a bag.

"He's on one of his trips," Joseph explained. "He does this often, and when traveling, he usually can't be reached. He came back early this morning, and we chatted during breakfast. I mentioned that the police had visited yesterday, and his whole demeanor changed. He said he needed to leave immediately. He didn't give any details—just packed and left. Is Vivek in some kind of trouble, sir?"

Anand's frustration was palpable. It seemed Vivek had been spooked by the police's earlier visit and fled. Quickly, Anand collected Vivek's mobile number and forwarded it to the cyber team, urging them to track the phone's location immediately. He then called Manoj and updated him on the situation.

"We need to search the area thoroughly," Manoj instructed. "He can't have gotten far." He immediately arranged for Vivek James's photo to be circulated to all patrol units and police stations across the state emphasizing the urgency of the search

Arjun contacted the cyber team for updates on Vivek's mobile location. They reported that the last known signal was from Kothamangalam, after which the phone appeared to have been switched off. They assured him they would notify him immediately if the phone was turned back on.

Police team launched a detailed combing operation, fanning out across the state. Hours ticked by with no sign of the suspect. Just as frustration was mounting, Arjun's phone buzzed—a breakthrough.

"He's turned his phone back on," the tech specialist reported. "The signal is coming from near the old factory on Willington Island. If you move quickly, we have a chance to catch him."

Arjun relayed the information to the team, and they sped towards the factory noting that the location is nearer to them than to Anand. They understood the importance of capturing the suspect before he had another chance to disappear. The sun was setting, casting long shadows across the landscape. The factory loomed ahead, a relic of a bygone era. They approached with caution; their senses heightened.

Inside, the factory was a maze of rusted machinery and dark corners. Arjun led the way, his flashlight cutting through the gloom. They moved silently; every sound amplified in the eerie silence.

Suddenly, a figure darted from the shadows. "There!" Arjun shouted, and the team sprang into action. The chase was on, their footsteps echoing through the cavernous space.

"Please," he pleaded, his voice trembling. "I didn't have any other option. I had to do it... to make things right. Those were paybacks for the sins of their past... from my future."

Manoj stepped forward; his tone steady yet commanding. "No more running. Just surrender. You don't have any other option. We need to know everything."

But the man, clearly unraveling, collapsed into a loop of frantic repetition. "Paybacks... sins of their past... from my future," he muttered, over and over, his words spiraling into incoherence as exhaustion and fear overtook him.

The night was deepening as they returned. The day had been long and exhausting, but they had made significant progress. The truth was within reach, and they knew they couldn't stop now. With their target in custody, they headed back, ready to unravel the final threads of the mystery.

Arjun pulled out his phone and quickly messaged the DIG: "We got him." He slipped the phone back into his pocket but hesitated, retrieving it again as a thought struck him. Dialing Kavitha's number, he waited, and the moment she answered, he said, "We got him, Kavitha. It's over. Thanks to you."

Kavitha's voice carried a mix of emotions—victory, sorrow, and simmering anger. "Did he say why he killed my Alex?" she asked, her words trembling slightly.

Arjun's chest tightened. "Not yet, Kavitha," he admitted gently. "But we'll know soon. I promise. Now, please try to rest. We'll have all the answers in a couple of days. Take care. Bye."

He ended the call, feeling the weight of her grief but resolved to deliver the closure she needed.

As the stars filled the night sky, Arjun and Manoj reflected on the events of the day. They had navigated their reality with determination and focus, and their efforts were beginning to pay off.

•••

Vivek was immediately taken to the doctor for his medical tests. After a thorough examination, the doctor confirmed that he was under the influence of a potent mix of drugs. At Arjun's request, the doctor administered injections to counteract the effects.

"This won't restore him completely right away," the doctor explained, "but it should reduce the drug's impact by at least 40%. If he gets proper rest, I expect he'll be much closer to normal by tomorrow afternoon."

Once the procedures were completed, they headed back to the station. He was made to sit in the interrogation room. With time being critical, the team decided to attempt questioning him that same day, hoping to extract any valuable information without delay. However, despite Manoj's efforts, Vivek was unresponsive, and unable to provide coherent answers. Realizing that further questioning would be futile, they decided to let him rest. Vivek was escorted to a room within the station, where he was placed under guard with two officers assigned to ensure his security.

Meanwhile, the forensic team had returned, bringing with them a collection of evidence from Vivek's residence. Arjun instructed them to prepare a detailed report as a priority. Additionally, he instructed the forensic team to do a Rapid DNA analysis of Vivek and to compare that with the one obtained from the hair strand found in the envelope that Arjun had discovered at Alex's murder site.

Manoj had assembled a multidisciplinary team at the station, comprising members from the forensic, cyber, tech, and pathology units. Arjun handed over Vivek's phone, laptop, and the bag he had at the time of his capture, instructing them to conduct a thorough analysis without delay. He also tasked the cyber team with performing a deep dive into Vivek's call history and mobile location data from the past one year emphasizing the urgency of uncovering any crucial connections.

Despite the exhaustion from an incredibly long and grueling day, the team knew there would be no rest that night with so much work to be completed. Yet, the adrenaline of progress and the taste of nearing success fueled their determination, keeping them energized and focused.

Time flew by like a racing horse as the team worked tirelessly in the conference room, a hub of relentless activity. The air was filled with the rapid clicks of keyboards, the hiss of burners, and the distinct scent of chemicals. As the moon faded and the first rays of the sun pierced the horizon, it symbolized the slow but steady progress of a victory the team was inching closer to achieving.

CHAPTER 19

THE FINAL NAIL IN THE INVESTIGATION

Day 2 after the ultimatum from DIG

By 6 AM, the team gathered around the conference table, exhausted but ready to present their findings. Kavitha joined them, raising a few eyebrows among the team members. Sensing the unspoken questions, Manoj addressed them directly. "Kavitha played a crucial role in identifying the suspect," he said. "Her expertise might prove invaluable in extracting further information and evidence to close this case."

The updates began, each team sharing their analysis:

Cyber Team Findings:

- **Call Records:** Vivek's call logs revealed multiple calls to each of the victims, likely made to track their movements or confirm their identities.
- **Location Tracking:** Vivek's phone was detected at or near each murder site during the times the murders occurred. Additionally, there were two trips to Tamil Nadu, including a few days spent in T Nagar, assumed to be linked to the planning and execution of Sofiya Ahmed's murder.
- **Pre-Murder Period:** Before the killings began, his phone activity showed extensive travel within the state, especially to Allookkara multiple times. His phone's GPS placed him near

the site of each murder days or even weeks before the crimes occurred, indicating meticulous planning and surveillance. However, two significant out-of-state visits stood out—one to Sirkazhi in Tamil Nadu, where he stayed for 2-3 days, and another to Basaveshwar Nagar in Bangalore, Karnataka, where he stayed for nearly two weeks.

Tech Team Findings:

- **Laptop Analysis:** Vivek had conducted extensive searches on committing murders without leaving traces and had studied numerous novels and articles about poisoning.
- **Dark Net Activity:** He regularly accessed the dark web. By cracking Vivek's ID, the tech team discovered that he was in regular contact with the drug dealers, maybe for the purchase of drugs. He was also found to have purchased the formula for a poison designed to leave no identifiable traces in the victim's body. The poison could be created using easily available chemicals and medications.

Forensic Team Update:

A wave of disappointment swept through the room as the forensic team delivered their findings. The DNA profile of Vivek James did not match the killer's DNA profile obtained from the hair strand found at Alex's murder site.

"Forensic expert Sarah addressed the group. "This might not be the person we're looking for," she said cautiously. "However, given the overwhelming evidence against him, there's also a chance the mismatch is due to inaccuracies from the Rapid DNA analysis method we used. We had already sent the sample for detailed DNA profiling yesterday night itself to the State Forensic Science Laboratory. The results should arrive in maximum within tomorrow evening, and only then can we confirm."

The team felt a momentary setback, as though hitting a temporary wall in their progress.

Refusing to let the team lose momentum, Arjun stepped forward with determination. "We'll wait for the detailed DNA results," he said. "But in the meantime, let's focus on tightening all the other evidence. We need to ensure every piece of this puzzle is in place without any loopholes."

Just then, Arjun's phone buzzed. It was a call from the DIG, asking if they were ready to hold a press conference to announce the arrest. Arjun looked at Manoj, who shook his head in disagreement. Arjun responded firmly, "Sir, please hold off for now. I'll update you on the announcement shortly. We need to strengthen the evidence before making anything public. For now, let's keep this arrest discreet."

With renewed focus, the team returned to work, determined to make the case airtight while awaiting the crucial DNA results.

Arjun turned to Maya and Rajiv with clear instructions. "I need both of you to talk to Joseph Antony, Vivek's uncle, with whom he was staying. I've arranged for him to be brought here this morning—he should already be waiting in the reception area. Get all the details about Vivek's life, from his childhood up until yesterday. Have your reports ready by this evening."

Maya and Rajiv nodded, quickly leaving the room to meet Joseph.

Meanwhile, Manoj was reviewing Vivek's phone location history. "Take a look at these pre-murder trips," he said, pointing to the screen. "The trips to Allookkara were for obvious reasons. Both are out of state—Sirkazhi and Basaveshwar Nagar. They're definitely not vacation spots. Sirkazhi is a temple town, and Basaveshwar Nagar is a residential area in Bangalore. My gut tells me there's more to this than meets the eye."

Kavitha chimed in. "I'm not familiar with Basaveshwar Nagar, but Sirkazhi is known for the Vaitheeswaran Temple, famous for Nadi astrology. Honestly, there's not much else to see there."

Manoj frowned in curiosity. "Nadi astrology? What's that?"

Kavitha leaned forward, explaining, "The Vaitheeswaran Temple is renowned for its ancient palm leaf manuscripts, which are said to contain the destinies of individuals, written thousands of years ago by sages. The astrologers, called Nadi readers, match your thumb impression to a set of leaves and read out details about your life—your past, present, and future. It's incredibly detailed, sometimes even mentioning specifics about past lives."

She continued, "The temple has become the center of an entire ecosystem. Most of the villagers there make their living from Nadi astrology. You'll find around a hundred reading centers scattered around the temple, with people visiting from all over the world for their readings."

Her voice dropped slightly as she added, "There's also a strange rumor tied to it. They say you can only reach the temple and have your reading done when you're destined to. Even if you plan to visit, something will prevent you from going unless it's your time."

The room grew quiet as the team absorbed this new layer of mysticism and its potential connection to Vivek's trip. The significance of his visit to such a place was becoming harder to dismiss.

Meanwhile, something clicked in Arjun's mind. Kavitha's mention of the temple and its association with Nadi astrology rang a bell. His face lit up with a sly, knowing smile—the kind he wore whenever a new idea struck him.

Without wasting a moment, he called Abhay Gupta, IPS, the head of the Special Investigation Team. Briefing him on the situation, Arjun requested two officers to be dispatched immediately—one to Sirkazhi and another to Basaveshwar Nagar. Knowing Arjun's instincts were rarely wrong, Abhay approved without hesitation.

One of the officers, Rahul, already stationed in Bangalore on another assignment, was rerouted to Basaveshwar Nagar immediately. The second officer, Ronald, boarded the earliest flight to Coimbatore, planning to continue to Sirkazhi with support from the local police.

The gears were now in motion, with the team following this new lead with renewed focus.

•••

Rahul arrived at Basaveshwar Nagar around 9:30 AM and headed straight to the area where Vivek's phone had been traced for nearly two weeks. With a team of ten local police constables, they began a systematic search, showing Vivek's photo to everyone they encountered. They left no stone unturned—shops, offices, street vendors, and homes—all were canvassed in their search for leads.

Hours passed with little progress until one of the constables reported a breakthrough. A shopkeeper recognized Vivek's photo and directed them to a nearby spiritual healing center named **Sanjeevanam Spiritual Healing & Rejuvenation Centre**.

Rahul rushed to the location and introduced himself to the practitioner in charge. The man, middle-aged with calm but weary eyes, seemed visibly unsettled as he began recounting his encounters with Vivek.

"Vivek was a deeply troubled soul," the practitioner said, shaking his head. "He came here seeking relief from years of unbearable mental torment. He'd been plagued by this agony for five or six years, unable to lead a normal life. Sleep was impossible for him—every time he tried, he was haunted by vivid nightmares or, as he described them, visions. He spoke of a girl being brutally killed during a ritual, performed by priests and involving seven others. These dreams consumed him."

Rahul listened intently, his notepad filling rapidly with notes. "Did he ever explain what he believed these visions meant?" he asked.

The practitioner sighed heavily. "We performed a soul memory retrieval process as part of his treatment. The results were... unsettling. He was convinced that in a past life, *he* had been that girl—the one sacrificed in the ritual. The revelation only worsened his mental state. He came here hoping to find peace, but instead, it seemed to unearth more pain."

Rahul frowned. "What did you do to help him?"

"We offered him various healing techniques—meditation, energy balancing, therapy sessions for almost two weeks—but nothing seemed to work. He kept fixating on one thing: the need to 'balance the scales.' He believed he had to make amends for the betrayal and violence of the past. He refused to let go of it. By the time he left, he was almost unhinged, consumed by the idea that only he could restore justice."

Rahul leaned forward, his voice calm but probing. "Did he ever mention who he thought the seven people were? Or what he planned to do?"

The practitioner hesitated, a shadow of guilt crossing his face. "No, he never mentioned specific names, but... he did talk about tracking them down. He said he could feel their energies like their presence in this life was linked to his torment. He believed that if he didn't act, the cycle of pain would continue."

Rahul thanked the practitioner and requested access to any records or logs from Vivek's sessions. The practitioner agreed reluctantly, handing over detailed notes and reports from their time with Vivek.

Rahul immediately forwarded all the information to Arjun and Manoj.

•••

Meanwhile, Ronald had reached Sirkazhi by around 1:30 PM. Guided by the local police, he delved into the labyrinthine world of Nadi astrology centers around the Vaitheeswaran Temple. Each center was a modest setup, filled with the aroma of incense and the hushed murmurs of seekers waiting for their destinies to be unraveled. Armed with Vivek's photo, Ronald visited one reader after another, but most shook their heads, claiming they didn't recognize him.

At the 21st center, an elderly man with sharp, penetrating eyes looked at Vivek's photo and immediately stiffened. "Yes, I remember him," he said, his voice steady but tinged with curiosity. He motioned for Ronald and the officers to sit as he reached for his meticulously organized records. After flipping through several pages, he pulled out a file labeled with Vivek's name and a CD marked "Vivek James." Placing on his headset, he listened intently to the recording for 5-10 minutes before stopping.

"He came to me a few months ago," the reader began, his gaze never leaving the records. "He sought answers about his past lives. The palm leaves revealed a life burdened by betrayal. His past life readings revealed that he was a girl whose life ended while she was still very young, during a ritual, may be a sacrifice for selfish needs. He was obsessed with this girl's death—claimed it was still haunting him. He believed this was the root of the torment he felt in this life."

Ronald felt a chill creep up his spine as he carefully jotted down the details. "What else did he say?" he pressed.

The reader paused before replying. "He spoke of visions—dreams that haunted him. He was desperate, almost frantic, to understand their meaning. The leaves indicated a connection to several individuals, tied by betrayal and unresolved debts of the soul."

Ronald thanked the man, took photos of the relevant records, and immediately forwarded the details to Arjun.

•••

Back at the station, Arjun and Manoj reviewed the reports from Ronald and Rahul. The puzzle was starting to come together, uncovering a narrative far darker and more twisted than they had expected.

The Nadi reader's account mirrored the soul retrieval practitioner's story, both pointing to a ritual and a girl's death. It was a chilling confirmation of Vivek's distorted sense of justice and retribution.

"The girl's death—the ritual sacrifice," Arjun said. "As we expected, he wasn't acting randomly—he believed he was settling karmic debts from a past life."

Manoj leaned forward; his expression resolute. "I think it's time we interrogate Vivek."

With the pieces of the puzzle finally aligning, the stage was set to uncover the full truth behind Vivek's dark and twisted motives.

•••

The chill of the interrogation room was a stark reminder of the gravity that hung over the case. Arjun and Manoj entered the interrogation room, the air thick with tension. Vivek sat across the table, his demeanor a mix of defiance and despair.

Manoj asked Vivek to confess. But Vivek remained in the same frantic state, his responses looping endlessly. Over and over, his trembling voice echoed in the room, repeating the same cryptic phrase: "*Those were the paybacks for the sins of their past, from my future.*"

His demeanor, however, suggested something beyond mere panic—it felt deliberate, as if he was refusing to confess rather than being lost in a frenzy.

Once Vivek calmed down, Arjun began, "We have all the evidence we need, Vivek," spreading the photos and documents on the table. "Your visits to Sirkazhi and Bangalore, your searches on the darknet, the poison formula, and witness identifications. It's over."

Vivek's composure shattered like glass under pressure. His defiance melted away, replaced by raw, uncontainable anguish. His hands trembled, his voice breaking as tears streamed down his face. "I was forced to do it," he choked out, each word heavy with torment. "You don't understand—I was *losing my mind*. It wasn't just nightmares. It was her face... her screams... every single moment. I could *feel* her pain like it was happening to me all over again."

He paused, clutching his head, his sobs reverberating in the room. "I needed it to stop," he continued, his voice shaking with desperation. "Every second of every day, I was haunted by what they did to her. The betrayal, the horror... I lived it. I *felt* the blade as if it cut through me. And they just stood there, watching, complicit."

Vivek's eyes, bloodshot and glistening, locked with Manoj's. "I couldn't sleep, couldn't eat. They were living their lives—smiling, thriving—while her death tore me apart again and again. I needed to make them pay. *They had to pay.*"

His tone shifted, darker now, yet resolute. "When I found them, it wasn't anger anymore—it was justice. They didn't just take her life; they destroyed her soul. And through her... mine."

The room hung heavy with his confession, each word cutting like a knife. The depth of his pain was palpable, his torment spilling out in waves. And despite the horror of his actions, the agony in his voice made it impossible to ignore the humanity behind his monstrous deeds.

As Vivek recounted the rituals, the connection to an ancient feud became clear. This was not merely a series of killings; it was an attempt to rectify past wrongs as perceived through the distorted lens of his beliefs. The victims were chosen not at random, but with deliberate intent, marked by a cycle of vengeance rooted deep in a cosmic battle of morality.

Arjun and Manoj pressed Vivek for details on how he committed the murders. His voice was eerily calm as he described each act with precision, recounting his methods step by step. The interrogation stretched late into the night, leaving Arjun and Manoj emotionally drained by the weight of his confessions.

By the time the clock struck 10 PM, all the remaining reports had arrived, including the detailed DNA analysis. The confirmation that Vivek's DNA matched the profile from the murder scene brought a wave of relief to the team. It was the final piece of evidence needed to make their case airtight.

With the evidence in place, it was time to prepare the final investigation report for submission. Arjun addressed the team, suggesting they head home to rest after their hard work. Kavitha also left the station. Meanwhile, Arjun, Manoj, Maya, and Rajiv stayed back, gathering in the conference room to draft the report.

Discussions ensued, filled with debates and meticulous attention to detail. Every aspect of the case was reviewed, ensuring the report was flawless and left no room for doubt.

By 1:00 AM, the final report was complete. Exhausted yet deeply satisfied, the team knew they had delivered a comprehensive document that tied the case together perfectly—days ahead of the deadline set by the DIG.

One by one, they dispersed, heading home with a sense of accomplishment. For the first time in weeks, they anticipated a peaceful night's sleep, knowing they had cracked the case and were ready for the big day ahead.

CHAPTER 20

THE COMPLETE PICTURE

The grand conference hall was silent, save for the faint shuffle of papers and the occasional murmur. Ministers, senior officers, press & media and dignitaries filled the room, their expressions a mix of expectation and tension. At the head of the room sat the DIG and IG, their eyes fixed on the team that had spent months untangling one of the most complex cases they had ever encountered.

The investigation team stood in a line at the front, their demeanor professional but proud. Arjun and Manoj stepped forward, their presence commanding the room's attention. Arjun, always eloquent, opened the briefing with an air of gravity.

"'Every truth has four corners: as a detective, it is our job to find them all,'" Arjun began, quoting Confucius. His voice resonated in the room, setting the tone. "Today, we present to you the complete truth—a truth that unveils a mind consumed by torment, vengeance, and an unrelenting quest for justice. It is not an easy story to hear, but it must be told."

He let the words hang for a moment before continuing.

Arjun turned to the screen behind him, where images and documents began to display. "Vivek James is the man responsible for these murders, and here is the evidence that led us to this conclusion."

- **Call Records:** "Vivek's phone records reveal multiple calls to every victim before their deaths. These weren't random—

it was surveillance, his way of ensuring they were who he thought they were."

- **Phone Location Tracking:** "Location data places Vivek's phone at or near every murder scene for weeks before the day of murder as well as at the exact time of the killings. The trail left no doubt about his presence."
- **DNA Match:** "From Alex Mathew's murder scene, we retrieved a hair strand sealed in an envelope. Detailed forensic analysis confirmed that it matches Vivek's DNA."
- **Digital Evidence:** "On Vivek's laptop, we found extensive searches on poisoning methods, untraceable murders, and historical cases of vigilante justice. He even accessed the dark web, purchasing the formula for a poison designed to mimic natural causes of death. Moreover, there were multiple folders we found in his laptop; each folder containing a chilling archive of the lives he had ended—pencil sketches, photographs, detailed profiles, their activities, routines, etc.
- **Eyewitness Testimony:** "Asif, the helper of Dinesh Menon, recognized Vivek's distinctive eyes and facial features, placing him at the scene of multiple murders."

Arjun paused, scanning the room. The weight of the evidence was clear, and the murmurs of disbelief from the audience confirmed the gravity of what they were hearing.

Manoj stepped forward to continue. The atmosphere in the room was thick with anticipation. His voice was steady but carried the gravity of what he was about to reveal.

"Each murder was meticulously planned and executed using a rare, untraceable poison that mimicked a natural heart attack. Vivek sourced the formula through the dark web and synthesized it himself using common chemicals, making it virtually undetectable during routine autopsies.

"As mentioned earlier, these killings weren't random. They were deeply personal. We learned from Vivek that the vigilante-like notes left at each scene were never intended for us or the public. They were messages for the victims—cryptic reminders of the guilt Vivek believed they carried for their roles in the ritual sacrifice that haunted him. He was certain they would recognize the meaning, even if no one else did."

Manoj took a deep breath, scanning the attentive faces in the room. "But, it is impossible to say whether all the victims had truly understood its meaning. Some might have grasped it in their final moments, a flicker of realization crossing their faces before everything went dark. Others, perhaps, never had the chance—left only with confusion, fear, or something worse. Anyway, here's how Vivek executed his plan."

•••

First Victim: Subhash Kumar

"Subhash Kumar, the owner of a private bank, was Vivek's first target. For weeks, Vivek had carefully observed Subhash and his family, noting every detail of their routines. He waited patiently, biding his time until the perfect opportunity presented itself.

On February 18th, that moment arrived. Subhash's wife, Vineeta, left for her daily yoga session, leaving Subhash alone at home. Vivek seized the chance. Disguised as a visitor looking for a friend's apartment, he approached Subhash's residence, his demeanor calm and composed.

Vivek's fabricated story and polite manner gained him entry into the house. Once inside, he engaged Subhash in casual conversation while surveying the space. Subhash's evening tea tray was already prepared, a ritual Vivek had observed repeatedly during his surveillance.

Vivek managed to create a momentary distraction. As Subhash looked away, Vivek swiftly laced the tea with the poison—odorless, tasteless, and nearly undetectable. Its slow-acting nature gave Vivek the time he needed to execute the final phase of his plan.

Before leaving, Vivek handed Subhash a folded piece of paper, without mentioning anything. On it was written the now-infamous message: *'Payback for your past, from my future.'*

Subhash, puzzled, unfolded the paper and read the words. Vivek watched closely, ensuring that Subhash saw the message while the poison began to take effect. The expression on Subhash's face—a fleeting moment of recognition and confusion—was exactly what Vivek had anticipated.

Vivek slipped away unnoticed, his movements precise and deliberate. Luck was on his side; no one saw him enter or leave the house. He left no traces, no evidence that could tie him to the scene.

After some time, Subhash collapsed quietly in his armchair, his death appearing as a peaceful heart attack. When Subhash's wife found him unresponsive, it appeared to be a peaceful death, masking the crime entirely. To the outside world, it was an unremarkable tragedy. But to Vivek, it was the first step in his dark mission—a calculated act of vengeance he believed was justified."

Second Victim: Alex Mathew

"Alex Mathew, a talented painter, was Vivek's second target. For weeks, Vivek had observed Alex's habits and routines. He learned that Alex often worked late in his home studio and had a particular excitement for unpacking new art supplies as soon as they arrived. Vivek waited patiently for the right opportunity to strike.

On March 15th, Vivek saw his chance. Understanding that Alex would be at home as he was not well, he carefully prepared his next move. Disguising himself as an anonymous sender, Vivek arranged for a courier to deliver a new painter's canvas to Alex's home studio.

This was no ordinary canvas. Vivek had embedded a small, nearly invisible fragment of a bee horn along the edge of the canvas border. Coated with a highly concentrated dose of the rare poison, the tiny shard was positioned to cause a minor, almost imperceptible injury to anyone unpacking the package.

When Alex received the package and eagerly opened it, his finger grazed the hidden shard, resulting in a barely noticeable prick. The poison, designed to enter the bloodstream immediately, began its deadly work.

As Alex set up the canvas, he noticed a chilling message written along the blank surface: *'Payback for your past, from my future.'* The cryptic words left him momentarily stunned. Vivek had ensured the message would force Alex to confront his guilt in the ritual that haunted Vivek. He was certain Alex's guilt would surface as he read the note before succumbing to the poison."

Moments later, Alex began to feel the effects of the toxin. Within minutes, he collapsed near his easel, clutching the canvas as if searching for answers. The scene appeared to be the tragic demise of an artist who had succumbed to a sudden heart attack while at work.

Vivek's meticulous planning left no trace of his involvement. The anonymous delivery provided no leads, and the poison, absorbed through the micro-injury, was undetectable during routine forensic analysis. Once again, Vivek had executed a flawless act of vengeance, certain that Alex had understood the message before his death."

Third Victim: Dinesh Menon

Manoj's voice carried a grim weight as he detailed the chilling execution of Vivek's third murder.

"Dinesh Menon, a seasoned reporter, was Vivek's next target. As with the previous victims, Vivek meticulously observed Dinesh's routines, learning his habits and vulnerabilities. Over time, Vivek uncovered a darker side to the otherwise respectable journalist—Dinesh secretly smoked marijuana, carefully sourcing it through an underground network to keep his habit hidden.

Vivek saw an opportunity and exploited it. After gaining insight into Dinesh's supply chain, Vivek managed to intercept one of the deliveries. Using the knowledge he had gathered, he tampered with the package, lacing the marijuana with his untraceable poison. The alteration was precise, ensuring the toxin would mix seamlessly with the substance and go unnoticed by Dinesh.

On April 8th, the tampered delivery reached Dinesh's home, appearing completely normal. Vivek, anticipating the moment Dinesh would use it, sent a WhatsApp message to Dinesh from an untraceable web-based application. The message contained his now-infamous quote: *'Payback for your past, from my future.'*

Later that evening, Dinesh indulged in his secret habit, smoking the marijuana. The poison worked swiftly, entering his bloodstream and triggering a fatal cardiac arrest. Vivek assumed that, as the toxin took hold, Dinesh would have seen the message and recognized its connection to the ritual that had haunted Vivek's life.

Dinesh's body was discovered slumped over his desk, an apparent victim of a sudden heart attack. The scene showed no signs of struggle or foul play, and the tampered marijuana went unnoticed by the initial investigators.

Vivek believed he had once again carried out a flawless, untraceable murder. But this time, unbeknownst to him, he had left behind subtle clues—a crack in his otherwise meticulous planning. This was the first thread we pulled to unravel the entire case."

Fourth Victim: Sofiya Ahmed

"Sofiya Ahmed, an IT professional in Chennai, became Vivek's fourth target. As always, Vivek began by meticulously tracking her daily routine, uncovering her habits and vulnerabilities. He discovered that Sofiya frequently stopped at a café near her workplace for coffee and confirmed that her husband, Ahmed Hussain, was away on a business trip on May 18th, 2023—leaving her alone and unsuspecting.

Disguised as a delivery staff member, Vivek infiltrated the café's backroom that day. Knowing which coffee cup was intended for Sofiya, he laced it with his signature untraceable poison, ensuring she would consume it without any suspicion. The poison was designed to act slowly, giving Vivek time to carry out the next part of his plan.

As Sofiya sipped her coffee and left for home, the poison began to take effect. By the time she arrived, Vivek had already sent her an email containing his now-infamous message.

Sofiya printed out the email, puzzled and disturbed by the cryptic words. She spent the evening staring at the message, trying to decipher its meaning, unaware of the toxin silently working within her body.

She passed away peacefully in her sleep, the poison triggering what appeared to be a natural heart attack. To Vivek, this wasn't merely a murder—it was a calculated act of vengeance, his version of delivering justice for the girl he believed was his previous incarnation."

Fifth Victim: Aparna Devi

"Aparna Devi, the prominent politician, was Vivek's fifth and final known victim. Vivek had been shadowing her for weeks, studying her schedule and movements. However, as a high-profile figure, Aparna was always surrounded by people—security personnel, aides, or supporters—making it nearly impossible to find a moment to strike.

Undeterred, Vivek followed her relentlessly, attending her public meetings and functions under the guise of a bystander, waiting for the right opportunity.

On June 20th, 2023, that opportunity presented itself. Aparna stopped at a busy restaurant for lunch during a trip from Calicut to Kannur. Vivek, posing as another customer, seized the chance. While passing by her table, he discreetly dropped the poison into her food. This wasn't a premeditated operation—it was an impulsive move borne of months of frustration and opportunity aligning at last.

Aparna, engrossed in conversation with her team, didn't notice anything unusual and consumed the meal laced with the untraceable toxin. The poison began its slow, deadly work as she left the restaurant and resumed her journey in her car.

Before departing the location, Vivek scrawled his cryptic note—*'Payback for your past, from my future.'*—and tossed it into the backseat of her vehicle. To Vivek, this note wasn't meant for the public or the police—it was for Aparna. He believed she would understand its meaning in her final moments, a direct call to the guilt he was certain she carried for her role in the ritual that haunted his life.

Aparna's driver, unaware of her deteriorating condition, continued the journey. Hours later, Aparna reclined in the backseat, appearing to rest. By the time they reached their destination, she was unresponsive—the poison had triggered what appeared to be a natural heart attack.

Once again, Vivek vanished into the crowd, leaving behind no obvious traces. His spontaneous but calculated act had claimed yet another life, furthering his dark mission of retribution."

Sixth Victim: Vijay Samuel

"Vijay Samuel, a prominent businessman, was Vivek's fifth target. Learning the routines, he discovered that Vijay frequently ordered meals from a specific restaurant near his office, a detail Vivek planned to exploit.

On June 20th, 2023, Vivek saw his opportunity. Disguised as a delivery staff member, he intercepted Vijay's food order while it was en route from the restaurant. Using the knowledge he had gathered during his meticulous preparations, Vivek laced the food with his untraceable poison.

The poison was designed to remain undetectable by sight or smell, ensuring that Vijay would consume it without suspicion. Vivek ensured the packaging was resealed to avoid raising any alarms and delivered the food to Vijay's office as though nothing was amiss.

Vijay, immersed in his work, consumed the meal unaware of the fatal substance it carried. As the poison began to take effect, Vivek sent his signature message to Vijay via an anonymous email.

Here also, the note wasn't intended for the police or the public—it was meant for Vijay. Vivek believed the cryptic words would force Vijay to confront his guilt for his alleged role in the ritual that had haunted Vivek's life.

Within hours, Vijay collapsed at his desk. By the time his colleagues discovered him, he was unresponsive, the poison having induced what appeared to be a sudden heart attack. The scene was clean, with no signs of foul play—just another victim in Vivek's twisted mission of retribution.

•••

Manoj's voice dropped slightly as he finished. "Each murder was carefully tailored to the victim's habits, routines, and vulnerabilities. Vivek believed he was delivering justice, ensuring that each of them would face the consequences of their actions in the ritual. As mentioned earlier, the notes were his way of forcing them to confront their guilt—messages meant solely for them to read before their deaths. He never expected anyone else to understand their meaning."

The room was heavy with silence, the chilling narrative leaving an indelible mark on everyone present.

The IG leaned forward, his voice breaking the silence. "And what was the motive behind these killings?"

Arjun stepped back in, his tone heavier now, as if he were about to reveal the darkest chapter of a novel.

"Vivek James wasn't always a murderer," Arjun began, his voice tinged with sorrow. "He was once a bright, promising child, excelling in academics and loved by all. But tragedy struck early—he lost both parents in an accident and was raised by his uncle, Joseph Antony."

Arjun gestured to the screen, where a photo of young Vivek appeared. "At first, he adjusted well. By all accounts, he seemed like a normal child. But when he turned thirteen, things began to change. Nightmares plagued him—visions of a girl being murdered in a ritual, surrounded by priests and seven shadowy figures.

"At first, the dreams were sporadic, but they intensified as he grew older. By seventeen, they became unbearable. He couldn't sleep, couldn't eat. Every time he closed his eyes, he saw her—her terror, her screams, her death. It was as if he was living her pain, over and over again. Gradually, the dreams became horrifyingly clear. He could see their faces—the seven participants and the priest leading the ritual. These faces haunted him, etched into his memory."

The room was deathly silent as Arjun continued.

"To escape, Vivek turned to drugs. But the addiction only deepened his torment. Despite multiple stints in rehab, funded by his uncle, the visions persisted. They consumed him, making him desperate for answers. He sought help discreetly, unwilling to share his struggles openly."

Arjun clicked to the next slide, showing photos of two towns to show Vivek's visits to **Sirkazhi's Vaitheeswaran Temple** and **Sanjeevanam Healing Centre in Bangalore.**

"At the Nadi astrology center, Vivek learned that in a past life, he was the girl from his visions—a victim of a ritual sacrifice. The soul memory extraction process in Bangalore confirmed these fears, revealing details of the ritual and the seven people involved. Vivek became convinced that these six of the seven individuals are still alive after an extensive search, and his torment would only end if he avenged her death."

Manoj added, "Despite being advised to perform rituals for peace, Vivek chose his own path. He sought out the reincarnated figures from his visions and killed them one by one, believing it would free him from his pain."

"He drew sketches of the seven individuals he had seen in his visions. These drawings became his obsession, his mission. From that moment, his life was dedicated to finding and killing them all, believing it was the only way to free himself—and to avenge the girl he believed he once was."

Arjun outlined the supporting evidence, while the slides on the screen showed the headers:

- **"Dinesh Menon's Report** revealed the connections between the victims, exposing their shared ties to an ancient ritualistic practice from two decades ago."
- "From **Allookkara Village,** multiple witnesses confirmed Vivek's repeated visits, always asking about the rituals and the tragic events that unfolded there, especially related to the death of that girl."
- **"Joseph Antony's Account:** His uncle described Vivek's descent into madness, his drug addiction, and his obsessive search for answers."
- **Reports from Sirkazhi and Bangalore:** "Both centers confirmed Vivek's claims of past-life torment and his determination to bring justice to the girl he believed he once was."
- **Vivek's Confession:** "During interrogation," Arjun concluded, "Vivek admitted to everything, repeating the same haunting words: 'Those were paybacks for the sins of their past, from my future.'"

The room remained silent, the weight of the case settling over everyone present.

The IG leaned forward, his voice cutting through the silence. "One question remains. How could Nadi astrology and soul memory retrieval reveal an incident from 20 years ago and connect it to Vivek?"

Arjun met his gaze, his tone calm yet firm. "There are forces in this universe that defy logic and science. Whether through spiritual connections, cosmic truths, or something we cannot yet explain, the evidence speaks for itself. Mysteries like these remind us of how much we still have to learn."

Arjun continued, "For the official records, we can attribute this to a case of a misunderstood personality disorder, exacerbated by exposure to random superstitious beliefs. However, the deeper truth is that these events might be connected in ways far beyond our current understanding."

The room erupted in applause. The ministers, IG, and DIG congratulated the team on their relentless search for justice. As the session concluded, the team filed out, their exhaustion replaced by pride.

Kavitha was waiting outside, her expression a mix of gratitude and relief. She congratulated the team with heartfelt warmth, her words laced with genuine appreciation for their dedication. As the others dispersed, she turned to Arjun, a soft smile on her face.

"Thank you, Kavitha," Arjun said, his tone sincere. For a moment, he hesitated, his curiosity getting the better of him. "I've been thinking about what the IG asked. How could the astrologer and the soul memory process uncover events from 20 years ago? And how did everything align so perfectly—Vivek's dreams, the ritual, the girl's death, his belief in being her reincarnation, and both the Nadi astrology and soul memory extraction confirming the same story? How could it all connect?"

Kavitha's thoughtful smile deepened. "Soul memory often reflects alternate universe experiences. Maybe the same events unfolded in one of Vivek's alternate lives. Or perhaps it's something beyond our comprehension—a convergence of dimensions, timelines, or energies. The universe is vast and mysterious, Arjun. There are phenomena we haven't even begun to understand."

Arjun listened, absorbing her words. He trusted Kavitha deeply and found comfort in her explanation, even if it didn't provide all the answers.

Kavitha hesitated before asking, her voice soft but steady, "Do you think we could be together here, as we are in Mohit and Neeta's universe?"

Arjun's expression turned gentle, though a flicker of sadness crossed his eyes. "Let's leave that to the other universe, Kavitha. Here, I have my passion and my path. And I'm already committed to my Divya"

Tears welled up in Kavitha's eyes and spilled silently down her cheeks. Yet, being strong and mature, she accepted his words with grace. She stepped forward, wrapping her arms around him in a warm embrace, and placed a tender kiss on his forehead.

Arjun, sensing the need to shift the mood, offered a subtle smile. "But, Kavitha," he added, his tone tinged with caution, "be careful with your invention. It's powerful but dangerous."

Kavitha nodded; her expression resolute. "I will. And you know that by now."

They walked together towards the team, their steps unhurried, as if savoring the last moments of a shared journey.

Arjun bid a heartfelt farewell to the team, expressing his gratitude and sharing a meaningful hug with Manoj. As he walked away, heading towards the airport, his thoughts were already turning to the challenges awaiting him in Delhi. Another mystery, another story, and another test of his resolve lay ahead.

And yet, for a fleeting moment, he allowed himself to reflect on the case that had just closed—lives intertwined by fate, justice, and the inexplicable forces of the universe.

EPILOGUE

Mohit's eyes sparkled with a mixture of amusement and contemplation as he entertained Neeta's hypothetical question. "In another universe?" he mused, leaning back against the soft cushions, his gaze fixed on a distant point as if picturing their alternate lives. "Well, if the multiverse theorists are to be believed, there could be countless versions of us, living out every possible choice."

He turned to face her, his hand reaching out to tuck a stray lock of hair behind her ear. "Maybe in one of those universes, I am not the black sheep of my family, but the golden boy celebrated and adored." A wry smile crossed his lips. "And perhaps you are not a secretary but the CEO of your own successful enterprise, calling the shots and steering the company to new heights."

Neeta laughed, the sound light and carefree, a stark contrast to the heavy, contemplative tone of their conversation. "And what if in one universe we are complete strangers, passing by each other without a second glance?"

"Impossible," Mohit replied instantly, his voice firm yet gentle, full of a conviction that warmed Neeta's heart. "In every universe, under every star, I would find you. Some things are constant, Neeta and my soul finding yours is one of them."

Mohit's words, spoken so earnestly, resonated with her deepest desires. Neeta felt her heart swell at his poetic words. With Mohit, she experienced a soul connection, unlike anything she'd ever known. The intensity of his understanding, his acceptance - it was as if he could telepathically navigate the depths of her psyche.

Overwhelmed, she threw her arms around him in a fierce embrace, clinging to his solid warmth as if it were the sole tether keeping her grounded. Wherever fate may lead them next, she knew her journey would be incomplete without his steadfast presence by her side.

When at last she found her voice, it was thick with unshed tears of adoration. "And I love you, Mohit, always."

No further words were needed as their lips met in a searing, all-consuming kiss. In that blissful eternity of a moment, their beings merged into a singular, infinite galaxy of eternal soulmates.

The universes around them faded into insignificance.

Jithin Roy

Jithin Roy was born in 1982 in the serene village of Kottappady in Kerala, as the son of Roy Varghese and Sarakutty CJ of the Puthukkunnathu family and the brother of Emie Roy.

After completing schooling at Vimalagiri Public School and Shobhana Schools in Kothamangalam, he earned an engineering degree in Electronics and Communication, from Mar Athanasios College of Engineering and later a postgraduate degree from Jaipur National University.

With a career spanning decades in the insurance industry, Jithin worked in India until 2012 before relocating to the UAE, where he continues to thrive professionally. Alongside his work, he remains actively involved in various social and community organizations.

He got married in 2009. His wife, Melby Mathew, and their three children—Evan, Mathew, and Sarah—complete his family.

A passionate storyteller from a young age, Jithin has always been captivated by crime investigation thrillers and extraordinary phenomena. His love for out-of-the-box thinking is reflected in his creative endeavors. During his college years, he scripted a drama, showcasing an early flair for storytelling. In 2008-2009, he penned a few songs, but it wasn't until 2019, at the age of 38, that he rediscovered his talent for writing. Observing the world around him, he began channeling his emotional reflections into compelling stories and poetry.

Since then, he has authored lyrics for six songs, scripts for various short videos, and four short films, some of which he also acted in. A collaborative short film he co-wrote and directed with a friend earned nine prestigious awards, cementing his place as a versatile creative force.

An ardent writer and poet, his debut Malayalam poetry collection, *"Ente Mounaksharangal" (My Silent Letters),* was well-received. He also contributed a heartfelt memory to the book *"Aa Naalu Varshangal" (Those Four Years),* a compilation of college life memoirs.

Jithin's foray into science fiction crime investigation thriller novels brings together his fascination with mystery, cutting-edge concepts, paranormal phenomena and human psychology. His stories are a blend of meticulous research, thrilling narratives, and profound emotional depth, keeping readers hooked until the last page. A firm believer in the power of determination, his mantra resonates through his works:

"It's not about who you are, where you are, or what you are, right now. Once you realize that, regardless of your age, you can conquer any heights with determination, and that's where life begins for you."

[A quote from Jithin's Script for 'The Survivor']